A Message Delayed

Tales from the Welsh Marches

by

Edward Tudor

Edward Tudor.

authorHOUSE®

AuthorHouse™ UK Ltd.
500 Avebury Boulevard
Central Milton Keynes, MK9 2BE
www.authorhouse.co.uk
Phone: 08001974150

First published by AuthorHouse 7/29/2008

ISBN: 978-1-4343-0671-5 (sc)
ISBN: 978-1-4343-0672-2 (hc)

Printed in the United States of America
Bloomington, Indiana

This book is printed on acid-free paper.

Though brothers may have private feud
They fight as one against the alien foe.
Books of Songs, Zhou Dynasty

Welsh Borders, in year of our Lord 1400

The tall young archer was standing on the top of the escarpment looking for a way down to the river valley. He pulled the hood of his cloak over his head as the chilling wind blew from the south-west. The view of the valley was magnificent; the autumn colours of the trees were a sight to see. From his vantage point he could see for miles up and down the river valley. The higher slopes were pine and the lower slopes were covered with deciduous trees, mighty oaks, silver birches and lines of willows along the river's edge in the bottom of the valley. There were meadows and even some cultivated fields on the floor of the valley. He drank in the scenery; the beauty was breathtaking.

The sun was getting low in the sky, like a great red ball. Evening was falling and it would be dark before he could make it across the river. He was undecided whether to make his camp on the top of the hill or when he got down into the shelter of the valley. The escarpment was too steep to take animals down through the trees. He could probably make it down on foot but he was looking for an easier way to travel – his pack was heavy and he was tired because he had been walking since dawn.

He was leaning out for a better view of the escarpment when he was hit by an arrow. It went through the back of his left shoulder turning his body with the impact, the arrowhead protruding high in the left side of his upper chest. A second blow struck him on the head; the bassinet under his hooded cowl saved him but the blow still stunned him and made him lose his balance. He could not stop himself from falling down the steep slope. As he fell he caught sight of three men with bows watching him fall. The glimpse was enough to etch their faces into his memory.

He plunged down the escarpment and bounced out into the air. The valley floor was over two hundred feet below the precipice where he had been standing. On the way down he struck an outcropping of rock and bounced further away from the cliff. He lost his grip on his bow as he twisted in mid-air, trying to grab onto the branches of the trees he was falling into. He grabbed the rough bark of a pine tree and tore his hands but as he threw himself against the springy branches he managed to break his fall.

He landed at the foot of the pine tree on a steep slope. His momentum carried him forward and he lost his balance again and continued to slide and roll down the slope towards the river. He landed heavily on his arrow bag and heard several of the arrow shafts snap with the impact. The arrow in his shoulder broke off and he cried out with the pain, but nobody heard him. His cry was carried away on the wind.

The archer finally came to rest in a bush near the edge of the forest, not far from the open meadow which led to the river. He could see the river Corve about half a mile away to the west and he knew the river Teme was beyond. He was shocked by the blow and by the fall but he was still just conscious. He pulled himself to his feet, fell down, tried again to get to his feet and steadied himself by leaning on a tree. What had just happened? The face of the archers who had shot him flashed through his mind. *Someone just attacked me. Why?*

His next thought was of escape. He did not know how badly he was wounded but he knew he needed to get away and from the pain in his chest and shoulder he knew he would not be able to shoot his bow or use his left arm to defend himself. Putting as much distance between himself and his attackers was what mattered now. He could leave working out why he had been shot until he was safe over the border in Wales.

The rain started again, coming down hard, and so he pressed on down to the river's edge. If he could get to the other side he could get across the border into the Marches of Wales and then he had a chance to escape before they found him, but only if he kept his head and kept moving. The wild country of the Welsh Marches would give him shelter until he could heal. He fell several times on the way to the river, and he crawled the last few yards on his hands and knees. By the time he got there he was covered in mud.

He lowered himself into the river and pushed out into the fast flowing water. He floated downriver using his good arm to steer himself across to other side. Dragging himself from the river he realised that his bow and his arrow bag were gone. He still had his belt but his eating knife had fallen from its pouch. He checked himself over and found he still had his falchion, his bollock dagger and his boot knife. His pouch was intact but his pack was still where he had hidden it before he went to reconnoitre the way down to the river. He could not go back and get it in the state he was in so he just headed west towards the river Teme further across the valley, using the trees for cover, moving from shadow to shadow. Several times he fell down but each time he pulled himself to his feet and kept walking.

He did not try to cover his tracks, he would do that later; now what he needed was distance between himself and his assailants. He was surprised they were not in hot pursuit considering how badly he was wounded. He stopped by the side of a tumuli so that he could tear the sleeve from his shirt. He bound the makeshift bandage round his wound and pressed on down into the next valley in search of a place to lie up for the night. The dark clouds were coming in from the west and the rain was likely to fall all night. With luck his tracks would be washed away but if he didn't find shelter he knew he could die of exposure in his weakened state.

Halfway down to the bottom of the valley he cut a stout staff from a sapling and used this to lean on as he continued on his way down to the river Teme in the bottom of the valley.

The rain was falling heavily now as he reached the river. He took off his boots and tied them around his neck. He stepped into the stream of fast running water using the staff to help him keep his balance. This was where he would lose his followers. He waded downstream where his footsteps could be easily seen on a muddy path. He left a clear trail that was easy to read until he reached the trees.

Now, the archer retraced his steps, going backwards into the stream. After leaving the false trail he waded upstream and climbed out on a rocky ledge where no tracks would be seen. Once he was well clear of the stream and far enough into the woods he put his boots back on. This was a struggle as he had lost the use of his left arm. He needed to get the arrow out and to have the wound cauterised but that would need a fire, and he could not risk a fire as it would show his position to his unknown enemy. Any light at night showed for great distances.

Using the staff to lean on he staggered on, heading in the direction he thought was west. As darkness fell he found a small glade and using some tinder from his pouch he lit a small fire. He had to use green wood to burn, however the smoke was dissipated by the surrounding trees. It was a risk he had to take; he had to get the arrow out of his shoulder.

He used some bark to heat some water to bathe his wound. He heated his boot knife in the flame until it glowed red. When it was hot and ready he bared his shoulder and grasped the bodkin arrowhead. He took a deep breath and pulled the arrow from the wound. His flesh tore and blood poured out onto the ground. He quickly used the heated knife to sear the wound on his back and on his chest where the wound was worst. He did not know which hurt more, the burn or the arrow removal.

He passed out with the pain. When he awoke he was shivering with fever and cold. He wrapped himself in his cloak and took a sip of the water he had heated. The fire had gone out so he covered over the small pit and spread leaves where his blood had poured out on the ground.

With the aid of his staff he pushed himself to his feet and walked slowly to a small clearing where he could look up at the sky. The rain had stopped and the sky was clearing. As the clouds thinned he could make out some of the stars and some of the constellations. He looked for the Plough. By connecting the stars at the one end and extending the line that joined them he found the North Star. From this he knew which direction he needed to travel. West for Offa's Dyke and the border and home.

Though he was weak, he knew he had to keep moving just in case his attackers decided to follow him to make sure that he was dead. He trudged slowly on through the night and as dawn came up he found a small copse to hide in. He found a place in among the trees, out of the wind, where he could sleep wrapped in his cloak. He lit no fire and hid himself deep in the undergrowth and prayed that they would not find him.

Ludlow Castle, Shropshire

"What do you mean you don't know where he is? Where is the body? There must be a body if you shot him, so where is it?" Lord de Grey of Ruthin demanded angrily. Lord Reginald de Grey was an very arrogant man not given to accepting failure from his men; he was used to getting his own way and usually had the support of Prince Henry of Monmouth, and Bolingbroke, the new King Henry IV. Lord de Grey had only contempt for the law and understood only the strength of his sword and the influence of his powerful friends. Lord de Grey was a powerful magnate in the northern Marches and the king was in his debt for his support in gaining the English throne.

The sergeant and his two men stood in the hall, silent, not wanting to answer their lord who was angry that the corpse of the messenger had not been retrieved. After the man had fallen down the escarpment they had returned to the inn when the rain started to fall heavily. Nobody could survive that fall, especially with two arrows in him, the sergeant had reasoned. They had returned to the castle at Ludlow only when the rain had started to subside.

"Well? I'm waiting for an answer. I want the message he was carrying, so you'd better get out there looking for him. I want it found now."

Gaspard, the sergeant, spoke up, "It'd be better to start fresh in the morning when we have daylight. One arrow took him in the back and the other in the head." He took a deep breath. "He fell into the valley; I saw his body hit the rocks on the way down; it would be a miracle if he survived the fall let alone the two arrows he had in him."

The look on Lord Grey's face showed he wasn't convinced.

Gaspard continued, "Even if he is still alive he's in no shape to travel very far in this weather and if he wasn't dead when he landed, he will be by the morning." He paused. "The weather is terrible out there, that's why we didn't follow him down into the valley after we shot him; the grade was too steep for the horses and I didn't want a horse with a broken leg. The ride round from the top of the escarpment into the valley would have been five or more miles and the horses were already blown from the day's searching."

Lord de Grey stood up and poured himself some more wine from a flask on the table. He took a sip and considered what the sergeant had said. He suspected the man had been shirking but had no proof and he needed the messenger found and he wanted the message he carried. His plans would be disrupted if the message got through to the Welsh lord. Glyn Dwr had been in favour with the old Earl of Arundel and that was something he wanted to change with the new earl.

The man, Glyn Dwr, was a lawyer trained in the Inns of Court in London and if he received the warning message de Grey would have to delay his plans to acquire the land in Wales they were in dispute over. He didn't have any rights to take the land but he would get away with it because of his friendship with the new king.

"Be sure you're in the valley by first light and that you've got him and the message he carries with me before noon. Don't fail me again or I'll have your worthless hide." With a wave of his hand he dismissed the sergeant and his men.

The three men trooped out of the warm hall and back down to the barracks in the outer bailey of the castle. Gaspard was angry but knew better than to take it out on his men. Once they were in the outer bailey he gave them their instructions: to have as many men as possible ready for the search at daybreak.

"They won't like it," said William, the older archer, whose arrow had hit the messenger in the shoulder. He was a stout man, a little above average height and with a portly stomach. He would rather be in his bed than chasing round the countryside looking for the corpse of a messenger.

"I don't care if they like it or not," snapped Gaspard angrily. "His lordship wants the bastard found and that's what we're going to do. Now go to bed and I'll see you in the morning."

The two archers watched the hunched figure of the sergeant walk away. The sergeant was not a tall man but he had a powerful stocky build and was know to be a dirty fighter.

The younger archer held his tongue until Gaspard had disappeared into the guardhouse. Once Gaspard was out of sight he said, "We don't really know if he was the messenger. Don't most messengers ride horses?"

"Usually yes, but he might have lost his horse and he was travelling light. He didn't even have a pack with him but he was armed with a bow and a falchion so I'd say he was either a messenger or a mercenary. Either way if he's dead that's no bad thing for us," said William, not wanting any competition for employment in Lord de Grey's service as he was getting older. His lordship was known to be ruthless in disposing of men he no longer needed. At William's age it would be hard to find another lord to serve.

"If he was just a mercenary passing through that means we could have missed the real messenger, does it not?" asked Jared, the younger archer.

"What you say is right but that's Gaspard's problem, we are just following his orders. So just keep your head down and you and I should be all right. His lordship is more interested in results than blaming someone and if he does blame someone then we just say we did as Gaspard told us to do. Come on now, let's get some sleep; tomorrow's going to be a miserable day hunting for that body, especially if this rain keeps up."

The two men retired to the warmth of the barracks in the outer bailey.

Gaspard was not a happy man. He had overheard the conversation as he stood in the shadows of the castle gatehouse. He had not considered that the man they had shot may not be the messenger. What if he was just a traveller or, as William had said, just another mercenary soldier looking for employment? He would really have a problem after what he had told his lordship. The boy had a point about the messenger having a horse but there had been so few horsemen seen in the last few days. The weather was partially to blame for that.

The worried sergeant turned and entered the gatehouse, welcoming the warmth of the brazier the guards kept going against the cold of the night. *Tomorrow will be a long day, especially if the weather doesn't improve,* he thought as he went to get warm by the guardhouse brazier. He warmed himself and then went to find his bed.

Cudlow Castle

Gaspard's mood had not improved overnight and at first light he was rousing the men from their warm bunks. Several men had saddled their horses and were standing waiting. Gaspard split his men into two parties: those with horses to search the far side of the river and those on foot to search the eastern bank.

Gaspard had already sent William and Jared with a long rope and a flag to show the point where the man had gone over the escarpment. He would take the men on foot and start his search from where the rope marked the man's fall. He was hoping this was going to be a quick job.

The last group of men came out of the barracks, some still stuffing bread and meat into their mouths as they came. They formed up into ranks ready to march, several muttering about the rain and fog. They pulled up their hoods and hunched into their cloaks against the weather. It had continued to rain all night and now a heavy fog had settled in the river valley and visibility was down to a few yards. This was not good weather to hunt a fugitive. The ground under foot was wet and slippery. Trudging cross-country was going to be hard and leg-sapping work. The meadows were all nearly water marshes and the tracks would either be muddy slides or small streams.

"The sooner we find the body, the sooner we can get back to our nice warm barracks," Gaspard said to encourage the men. "Jorge, you take a dozen riders over the bridge to the other side of the Teme and follow the bank up to see if you can find any sign of him, but I doubt if he got that far. If we find the body I'll send someone to call you back, so keep some men close to the river bank."

"We need to exercise the horses anyway so we'll ride along the western bank for a couple of miles. Just send someone down to the river so we know where we need to start our search," Jorge replied as he mounted his horse. He waved to his men and they walked their horses out of the castle gate.

Gaspard led his men out of the gate, round the castle and down a path towards the flat of the valley. The men slipped on the muddy path and more than one fell in the slippery mud, but within half an hour they were on the valley floor. Gaspard spread the men in a skirmish line as they walked towards the escarpment. It took them over an hour to find the rope that William had thrown down the escarpment as a marker. The men looked through the undergrowth but no body was found. There were few tracks left by the wounded man because of the heavy rain through the night.

Gaspard formed his men once again into a skirmish line, each man a bow's length from his neighbour, and they started to work their way from the cliff down towards the river Corve. The men grumbled but complied as they fought their way through the undergrowth, getting very wet in the process. The branches doused them in water as they brushed by. Soon every man was soaked to the skin and feeling rebellious. Gaspard thought, *This is not good for morale.*

It was not long before they found the tree the man had used to break his fall, but there was no body, just some broken branches. They found the steep slope where the man had fallen and landed on his arrow bag. The bag was found a few yards from the bottom of the slope, alongside several arrows lying on the ground.

"You didn't kill him then," commented one of the searchers and Gaspard rounded on the men to see who had spoken. He glared at the men but could not identify the speaker.

"He can't have got far after that fall and he has two arrows in him," muttered Gaspard almost under his breath. "Bastard!"

The fog in the valley was still thick so the men formed their skirmish line again and searched the woods down to the river bank. The fog got thicker as they got closer to the river. The men found themselves wading in water and several got stuck in the marshes of the meadow and had to be pulled clear with a rope.

Unfortunately for the hunters the river had risen and the man's tracks had been obliterated by the water. They could not find where the man had entered the river, but from the direction he had come he must have headed straight into the water. What should have been a short morning's work was turning into a full scale hunt. Gaspard sent a runner to say, *Have horses brought down to the river.*

Jorge and his men were sitting on the other bank watching Gaspard's men search the river bank for signs of where the man had entered the river. They were indistinct shapes in the fog. Jorge's troop sat on their horses, keeping their distance from the water's edge as the land was so boggy.

"Can you find any tracks over there? We've found his arrow bag. It looks as if he came down to the river but his tracks have been washed away by the rain," shouted Gaspard.

Jorge had his men dismount and look for signs of an injured man leaving the water, but the rain and the river had washed away any evidence of the man's passing. The search continued all morning but they found no body and no evidence of which direction the man had gone.

"If he fell into the river he could have been washed downstream. He could be miles away by now. He's probably drowned anyway," offered William, the older archer, as he walked up the edge of the river.

That was not what Gaspard wanted to hear just as he saw Lord de Grey riding along the valley towards him. His lordship did not look pleased as he rode through the fog.

Lord de Grey rode up to where Gaspard was standing. "Where is he then?" came the lord's curt question.

Gaspard held up the arrow bag. "We found this over there. He came down into the valley and it looks like he was heading for the river. The rain has washed out any tracks but we've searched both up and downstream and if he made it into the river he certainly didn't make it out."

"What you mean is the rain has washed away his tracks and you can't find his tracks because you didn't make sure and search for him last night when you could have caught him," snapped Lord de Grey. "Search every farm, hamlet and village from here to the border and find the man or his dead body. I want him dead or alive. Do you understand?"

"What if he didn't make it out of the river? He could be miles downriver by now or he could be stuck underwater somewhere," Gaspard said, knowing the search would not go down well with the men. They would not blame Lord de Grey, they would blame him, and Gaspard liked being popular with the men.

"Just find him! If you can't do it I'll find someone who can," Lord de Grey replied sharply to the sergeant.

"Yes, my Lord," Gaspard said, not wanting to lose his position. He started organising his men into groups: one to search the river banks; another two groups to search the nearby farms and villages. He called across the river to Jorge to search the route towards the border.

Soon men were scurrying off in different directions to continue the search. Gaspard watched as his men spread out. What if William was right and the man they had shot was not the messenger and what if he had been washed downriver? He looked about and sent one of his men to find a boat to drag the river. It would be time-consuming but it would have to be done if only to prove to his lordship that the messenger was really dead.

Lord de Grey sat on his horse and watched as Gaspard sent the men about their duties. The messenger wasn't important but the message was and he needed to have it so that he could discredit Glyn Dwr in the eyes of the king. However, he could not waste too much time searching because he needed to journey north to join King Henry in Scotland. The ambitious Percys wanted help in containing the Scots and the king needed to give it to ensure their support of his claim to the throne.

Will's farm, West of Cudlow

The young bowman woke. His shoulder was stiff and it ached like hell. His head hurt from where the arrow had hit his helmet. He took his time in getting moving, slowly getting warm by rubbing each limb and gently stretching his muscles. He took a sip of water from his flask and chewed a piece of dried meat he had in his pouch. He was soaked through and shivering with cold. He put his hand to his forehead and felt the heat; he was running a fever and was feeling very weak. He needed to find somewhere warm and dry to recover his strength. He knew that his wet clothes would kill him if he could not dry them, and soon.

It took him a few moments to recall where he was and what had happened to him. He stood up and brushed off his cloak. His wound was bad but he could not afford to stay where he was. He looked out from the cover of the trees to see if he was being pursued and was surprised to see no trace of pursuit. He might have dreamed his predicament but for the wound in his shoulder and the ache in his head.

The evening was coming and he needed some hot food as well a dry place to shelter for the night. He was just about to leave the copse when he caught a movement in the corner of his eye. Horsemen were coming over the brow of the hill and forming a skirmish line.

So someone was searching for him. He shrank back into the copse and waited, wishing he still had his bow. He vaguely remembered falling on his arrow bag but not much else about how he had escaped from his attackers. He did not know how far he had managed to travel from the ridge where he had been ambushed.

Tracks, he must have left tracks coming from the river. He peered out at the field the horsemen were crossing but could see no tracks. He thought the only reason they were not following his tracks was they must have been obliterated by the wind and rain, therefore it was safer to stay where he was and make no movement. That way there would be no new tracks for his hunters to find.

The horsemen crossed the field and stopped as they reached the woods.

A large horseman signalled the others to come together in the lea of the copse out of the south-westerly wind. When they were all in a group the leader asked, "Has anyone seen any tracks or found anything showing the messenger came this way?"

There was a general shaking of heads and a few groaned no's as the men pulled their cloaks around them for protection from the weather. They were all wishing they were back in barracks near a warm fire.

"If he was as badly wounded as Gaspard said I don't think he would have got across the river let alone this far. But we'd best be thorough or his lordship won't be pleased if he gets away. Two of you go to that farm and three to the hamlet over the ridge. We'll meet in the inn in an hour. The rest of you ride through the woods and see if you can find any tracks or sign of the messenger," said the leader.

"It seems a lot of fuss for a messenger who's probably dead and if he isn't he's badly wounded so he won't be delivering any messages," commented one rider as he rode away with his companion to search the farm.

"If he has any sense he'll be hiding in a nice warm barn," said another.

"Look, if Lord Grey wants him dead then that's what we do. If Gaspard had done the job right last night we wouldn't need to be out here. But the stupid lazy bastard shot him and then went off to the inn instead of finishing the job. If you want to blame anyone blame him."

The young archer moved quietly back into the undergrowth as the horsemen split up into their groups to carry on their searches.

He returned to where he had slept and covered the area with some branches. He brushed the grass and sprinkled some autumn leaves over the floor of the copse.

The horsemen searching the copse were not very diligent as they were cold and wet and had thoughts of a warm inn on their minds, not a cold fugitive who was hiding in the undergrowth wrapped in leaves.

The sky was darkening once more and it started to rain again. From his hiding place, the archer heard a hail shouted and the horsemen in the copse turned and rode off at a canter. The fugitive watched them ride off from where he lay under the trees in the undergrowth.

As they went he counted them. There were five cantering across the field and two more were waiting by the farm. As soon as the last rider arrived at the farm they all set off down the road to the west towards the hamlet.

The fugitive sat at the base of a tree and considered what he had learned. Lord Grey wanted him dead and one rider had described him as a messenger. But a messenger for who? What was the message? And the final thing: the man who had shot him was named Gaspard.

Gaspard was the one who had shot him, so he owed him. Caradoc considered his predicament. If he went to Lord Grey he would probably be killed on sight so that was not an option because he had heard that the Marcher lord was a pitiless man and was not a friend to anyone Welsh. So that left the only other option of escaping over the border into Wales. He was still several miles short of the border and just crossing it would not definitely mean safety.

As the farm had been searched already that would be a good place to spend the night and possibly steal some food. He wondered if they had any horses; escape would be easier than on foot, especially with his wounded shoulder.

As the sun sank below the skyline the archer made his way carefully across the fields to the farmyard, listening out for the return of the horsemen. He was careful to leave no tracks as he moved towards the farm. He peered round the wall of the barn and, seeing no one, he slipped inside.

He looked up at the hay loft but that was such an obvious place to hide he rejected it immediately. As he was looking round the barn he saw a water bower in the yard so he took the opportunity to fill his flask. He thought of the riders at the inn and his stomach growled. He went back towards the barn and noticed a small smithy at one end. He went in and looked around. Without a bow and with his left arm out of use he could use another weapon, and the best thing would be a sling shot. He had not used one since he was a boy herding his father's sheep but he was sure he could still use one to good effect and it would be better than nothing.

As he was looking round the smithy he found what was left of someone's lunch, a piece of meat pie. The archer scooped it up and ate it as quickly as he could, cramming the food into his mouth and swallowing almost without chewing. The food was soon gone but he did feel better. He continued his search and soon found what he was looking for, some leather and some leather thongs. He cut a piece of the leather and selected four thongs. If he took more it would be noticed and he did not want the farmer to discover his theft. He returned to the barn and hid himself in a dark corner and set about making a sling and a pouch for the stones he would use as ammunition.

Lightening lit up the sky and thunder rumbled to the west. The sky was dark and night fell but at least he was under shelter and out of the wind and rain. Even though the barn had no doors, the hay and stalls kept the westerly wind off him and he was able to hang his cloak up to dry. He took off his clothes and rubbed himself dry with some sacking. Once warm he covered himself with some more sacks to keep him warm while his clothes dried. He used some more sacks to make a bed and once he was comfortable he fell into a dreamless sleep.

He was awoken in the morning by the clattering of hooves in the yard. He pulled his cloak off the railing where it had been drying and threw the sacks back on the pile he had taken them from. He went into a stall, picking up the rest of his clothes as he went, and covered himself with straw to hide. The straw was prickly against his skin but he had to put up with the irritation or be discovered. Hiding under the straw the wind soon penetrated his hiding place and he began to lose the precious warmth he had gained overnight in his bed of sacking.

The large horseman he had seen the previous day entered the barn with a smaller man following him. The smaller man was complaining, "Your men searched the place last night and found nothing. If you told me what you are looking for then maybe I could help." The smaller man looked round his barn and said, "I cannot spend all my time clearing up after you and your men."

The tall horseman named Jorge looked round the barn and considered the farmer. He knew that some of the border families had close links and even relatives on the other side of Offa's Dyke and it was probably not a good idea to be very trusting of the local population.

"We're looking for a man who has something belonging to Lord de Grey of Ruthin and his lordship wants it back. There may even be a reward for anyone who helps us find him. I understand he's badly wounded in the shoulder and in the head. We found his blood where he fell off the cliff overlooking the river Corve."

While he had been talking his eyes had swept the barn, looking for anything out of place. He couldn't see anything, though the barn was tidier than most he had seen. He went to the ladder and climbed into the hay loft. There was a scrape as he drew his sword from its scabbard. He prodded various sheaves of hay and then climbed back down from the loft.

"If you see anyone or you find any sight of a wounded traveller going towards the border let me know at the castle in Ludlow. Ask for me at the gatehouse. My name is Jorge; I'm Lord de Grey's Sergeant-at-Arms," he said, trying to impress his importance on the small balding farmer.

The farmer followed Jorge back out to the yard and the archer stayed where he was until he heard the hooves moving away and getting softer with the increasing distance. He was still lying there thinking about what to do next when he heard the farmer return. "You can come out now, they've all gone."

The archer crawled out from his hiding place and stood up. "How did you know I was here?"

"Those sacks were not piled as tidily and the straw you were under was flatter yesterday," came the sharp reply.

"You could have handed me over to Lord Grey's man and claimed your reward," said the archer, incredulous that the man had forgone a reward.

"Yes, I could, but I wanted to know who was being chased and why. If you are from over the border then I have friends there and if you are related to them they might not be my friends any more. The other reason is that I don't like Lord Grey; he's an arrogant bastard and his lands are in the north and Cheshire so if I turn you in it would be to Shrewsbury where Prince Henry has a garrison. The reward from the prince should be better than one from his lordship, who I happen to know is not over keen on opening his purse-strings. So why are they chasing you?"

"That's what I would like to know myself. I was walking back from Oxford with a small pack of trade goods for my mother to the Vale of Ceri. I hid my pack and went to look for a way across the river when I was shot in the head and shoulder. I lost my bow and my arrow bag and I fell down the hill. I'm lucky to be alive. I managed to float across the river and I made it to the copse across the fields and I got to your barn late last night," the young man explained.

He continued, "I overheard some of the horsemen talking and they are looking for a messenger. I don't know who the message is from or who it's going to but I do know I don't have it. If I give myself up to Lord Grey he probably won't believe that I am not this messenger and will kill me anyway. So I was going to make for the border and get back to my family in the Vale of Ceri."

"Put your clothes on and come to the house and we'll have a look at that shoulder and get you some food. I'm Will, what's your name?"

"Caradoc ap Ednyfed," the young man replied.

"Well, Caradoc of Kerry, we'd better get you fixed up and on your way." And he led the way across the yard to the farmhouse.

The kitchen was warm and smelled of baking bread. Caradoc was soon feeling much better. The farmer called his wife and she dressed his wounds, draining out some puss, putting a poultice on to draw any more poison out. After she had tended the wound she brought him a hot bowl of mutton stew with fresh bread arid a tankard of small ale.

Caradoc thanked her and set about the food as he was very hungry, having eaten very little for two days. He was surprised to see how much younger than her husband she was. There were no children that he could see and Caradoc wondered if they had been hidden because of the horsemen. Soon steam was rising from his clothes as they dried in front of the fire.

The woman took her husband to another room and Caradoc could hear the low murmur of voices. They were obviously discussing him and the predicament he had put them in. He finished his ale and sat drowsily by the fire. He did not hear the farmer return and stand over him.

Caradoc slept and the farmer threw a blanket over him. Will looked down at the boy and wished he had a son like him to leave the farm to when he died.

Kate, the farmer's wife, said, "Go now and get his lordship's men while he's asleep. You can claim the reward."

"That would not be a wise thing to do," replied Will. He had lived in the Marches all his life and knew the value of having allies on the other side of Offa's Dyke. Early warning of a raid or of an army passing through could be invaluable for hiding stock and food stores and any other valuables. His wife came from much further east and had had fewer dealings with the Welsh and did not understand the ways of border life.

"But that man said there would be a reward," she insisted.

"For Jorge, maybe, but not for us. If I give this boy to Lord Grey and the boy is executed then I will have enemies on the other side of the border. They probably won't be able to take their revenge on Lord Grey but they will know about us and then the raids will start. Do you remember Robert, who had the farm over towards Clun? He had a disagreement with a Welsh family and he was raided so often that he lost all his livestock so the FitzAlans took his land away and gave it to another man." Will emphasised, "He lost his wife and family, his land and now he's a journeyman in Shrewsbury. I don't want that,

I want to be on my own farm. I don't want to work for someone else or live in a town."

Kate continued her protest. "But if his lordship found out you'd hid this man he'd kill you too. When you see him you could ask for his protection from the Welsh."

"How little you know, woman. Who is going to tell Lord Grey? You?"

"No, of course not," she protested.

"This Lord Grey has lands in Cheshire and the north. He will move back there in a few days. When he goes so will his men and what protection would I have then? Sir Edmund can't protect me even if he wanted to. He's hard enough pressed to protect his own lands and he has castles and retainers who are fighting men." Will continued, "The Welsh don't forget a wrong and this boy and his family will remember the favour we've done him."

Will continued his explanation. "Also, if I have protection from Lord Grey I will be saddled with some of his lordship's men who I will then have to feed and they will get in the way of running the farm. Our neighbours will ask why we have Lord Grey's men here and that will lead the boy's family to us as well. So our best way out of this is to keep quiet and say nothing to his lordship and his men and let the boy slip away. If he gets caught closer to the border then that's not our fault, we tried to help him. My love, the Welsh are always here but this Lord Grey will soon be gone and Lord Arundel will be back with the Mortimers. So I am going to patch the boy up and send him on his way, and say nothing to nobody."

She sulked and she knew he was not doing the right thing. Why was he so paranoid about the Welsh?

He answered her unspoken question.

"If I lose my friends over the border it will be our farm that's raided and our stock that will be stolen. Not only that, the boy's family will want revenge and it will be you and me that they kill, not Lord Grey and his men. Do you understand me?"

"But what about the reward?" she protested, her greed getting the better of her.

"Jorge lied. Lord Grey might reward Jorge but he won't give me a single groat. I know of him from the market in Shrewsbury. He's a tightwad and he's greedy for land. He's very powerful and has influence at the king's court and with his son, Henry of Monmouth, but we are not his tenants and he will just take what he wants and have no thought of us or anyone who is below his rank. In the borders we have to be pragmatic about dealings with the nobility. Look at the trouble the Mortimers got into with Edward the Second and his son. It cost the earl his head. But they didn't suffer as we farmers did."

The farmer's wife was still not convinced but she held her piece. As soon as she could she would go to the castle and claim her reward. She would save her husband from himself and his fear of the Welsh.

The next morning Will packed some food for Caradoc, who was feeling much better after his night's sleep by the fire. He gave the young archer directions and told him of places where he could hide and of people who would help him.

The farmer's wife gave him a spare poultice but she was glad when she saw him top the rise on the road to the west. Caradoc still felt weak but was much recovered in his dry clothes and with some food in his stomach.

Kate watched Caradoc make slow progress down the road. As she watched him she realised that she could get to the castle and tell them before he reached the border. She would get the reward and her husband would not be blamed for his capture.

As soon as she could she put together a basket of produce to take to Ludlow. She would go to the castle and claim her reward from Jorge and Will would be none the wiser. She wondered how much the reward would be. She was excited at the prospect of what she would buy at the next fair. Perhaps she could get Will to take her to Shrewsbury where there was so much more choice with all the shops there.

Clun to Offa's Dyke and the Vale of Ceri

Caradoc set a good pace considering his condition and was moving west along a broad track towards Clun, skirting north around Hopton Castle. He planned to circumnavigate the small town and make directly for Offa's Dyke. He was aiming to get across the dyke south of Montgomery, staying well away from the castle that dominated the Severn Valley. He heard some horses travelling along the road so he took to the woods that covered Black Hill. Once the horses had passed he waited for some time to see if there was a rear guard. He was just about to start walking again when a rider came cantering along the road. Caradoc shrank down into the bushes and waited until the rider was out of sight before he cautiously took to the road again.

As Caradoc skirted round Black Hill he saw some hares running in an open meadow. He took out the sling he had made and put a stone into the pocket. He wound one of the slings thongs around his hand and then held the other strand to his palm with his middle finger.

He crept closer to his prey and then suddenly stood up, whirled the sling in a vertical loop and released. The missile flew through the air and just missed the large hare he had been aiming at. No sooner had he missed but the hares vanished from sight.

Caradoc squatted down, depressed at his missed throw. He rolled the sling up and hobbled back to the road to continue his trek on towards the border.

Just before he got to Clun he saw a flock of sheep being herded west along the drover road. Caradoc thought he would lose his tracks in with those of the sheep and if he was lucky the herders might help him. He walked as fast as he could to intercept them on the track. The head shepherd was riding ahead of the flock, and watched impassively as Caradoc struggled to get ahead of the sheep.

"I'm heading for the border. Can you help me?" Caradoc asked as the rider came close.

The leader looked down from his horse and saw the blood on the front of Caradoc's tunic. "Had some trouble with the English, have you?" he asked in Welsh.

Caradoc nodded and answered in the same language, "They shot me in the shoulder and the head but I don't know why, and I didn't stay to ask them."

"That's the English for you. Do you think you can sit on a horse?"

"I don't know about ride but I can hang on if someone can help me up."

The man called to one of his men who was leading a string of horses. The man rode up and rigged a rope halter for Caradoc. He roped other horses together so that they would be easy for Caradoc to manage.

"If you can ride bareback and bring the horses with you that will free up, ahhhh." He paused, not wanting to give his comrade's name. "He can then help with herding the sheep. And the faster we move the better, if you understand my meaning."

Caradoc nodded his understanding and the leader dismounted and helped Caradoc up onto the horse. He passed him the lead ropes for the spare horses and set him off ahead of the flock of sheep.

"Don't get too far ahead of us; we need to keep in touch, especially once the sun has gone down," said the leader.

The leader led the men off, herding the sheep so the pace was not so fast that Caradoc's wounds were agony, but certainly faster than his best walking pace. He rode on with the horses, trying to sit straight. He noticed there was a rider about half a mile behind the main group. He kept looking over his shoulder until the leader said, "If anyone comes after us, he'll let us know. Just concentrate on keeping up and staying on that horse."

They rode on through the afternoon. The rain had stopped but the ground was still very wet and this had turned the road into a quagmire of mud. Although the progress was slow they kept going into the night without stopping and slowly they ate up the miles to the border. Caradoc looked up at the stars and found the constellation Ursa Major, the Plough; by joining the two end stars he was able to find Polaris, the North Star. They were definitely heading west and that meant that they were getting closer to the border. It was rough country and the horse's motion jarred his wound but at least the pain kept him awake and alert.

The leader checked on him every half hour to make sure Caradoc was still awake and alive. He could see the young man was hanging on and he was getting very weak but he owed it to the rest of his men to just keep going. He could not risk the safety of his men for this stranger, even if he was Welsh.

"If you need to stop, just call out. We'll be over the Mercian's Dyke soon and that means the English will have second thoughts about following us," he said to encourage Caradoc.

Caradoc swayed on the horse's back and nodded, then realising the man could not see him, he said, "Thank you, I'll feel better once we are back in Cymru. Meeting you has saved my life, I think."

The man laughed. "I wouldn't want to see a fellow Welshman die on the wrong side of the border. So they shot you without warning, did they?"

"Yes, I lost my pack, my bow and my arrow bag. I had to run for it with just what I was wearing. I thought they'd chase me but they didn't follow me until the following morning. I got the arrow out and a farmer's wife put a poultice on it. So I've been lucky so far. If I can get home to Ceri I think I'll survive."

The man smiled at the youngster's determination. "Just hang on and we'll get you there but we'll have to leave you once we get to the vale. We go south to Rhaeadr Gwy and we have to be at a meeting place by noon tomorrow."

They plodded on in silence, ever westward towards the salvation of Offa's Dyke and the safety of the wildness of mid Wales.

Ludlow Castle

Ludlow Castle was a very strong fortress as well as the centre of power and administration for the central Welsh Marches. It had never been taken by force and it held a strategic point in the centre of the Marches in lower Shropshire. It was close to Wigmore Castle, the home of the Mortimers, and was also near the guild town of Shrewsbury. It was an ideal place to govern the Marches without actually being in Wales. The castle stood high on the ridge overlooking the river Teme, in the centre of the market town of Ludlow.

It took Kate, the farmer's wife, a good two hours to get to Ludlow, and that was after she had persuaded her husband Will of her need to go to the town behind the castle to get some supplies in exchange for the produce in her basket.

She crossed Ludford Bridge and entered the walled town by Broad Gate, which was the main entrance to the town from the south. She climbed Broad Street until she got to King's Street. She turned left along the High Street and entered Castle Square.

She approached the gatehouse just after noon and was wary at being seen at the huge grey fortress in the clear daylight. It took her some time to pluck up the courage to walk across the town square to the main gate in the curtain wall. She rapped on the ironbound gate and asked the guard if she could speak to Jorge.

The guard went in with a smirk on his face. The poor doxy wouldn't get much out of Jorge, of that he was certain. He knew of the sergeant-at-arms and knew he was a ladies' man. He had only been in Ludlow a few days and Jorge had a woman already.

She waited and waited and eventually the guard returned and took her into the guardhouse. There she was told to sit and she sat on a bench to wait. She could see the day was drawing to a close as the room got darker and the lamps were lit. She needed to be on her way back to the farm or be stuck in the town overnight. She was starting to panic.

Eventually Jorge arrived back from his day's searching for the messenger. He handed his horse to one of his men and took the message from the guard. He looked at the woman but could not place her. Had he tupped her in the local hostelry when drunk? He didn't think so.

"What do you want of me?" he demanded rather harshly.

Kate stood up and tried to be bold. "The reward for the man you are chasing."

This immediately focused his attention. "What! You know where this man is?"

"I saw a wounded man walking west this morning towards Clun. He had a staff, no pack and was obviously in pain, and his left shoulder was padded as if it was bandaged. It sounded like the man you described to my husband at our farm yesterday."

"Your husband? Which farm was that – we visited several yesterday."

Kate described the location of the farm and Jorge called to his men to get fresh mounts. All of a sudden there was a clamour of action as men rushed to get ready to ride out from the castle.

Kate went to Jorge's side and tugged at his sleeve. "Where's my reward?"

"Don't worry, you'll get your reward but first I have to arrest him and verify this man's identity. You'll get your reward then when we have him in captivity," he said with a smirk as he peered down her cleavage.

Jorge turned to the guard. "Keep this woman here until I return."

Kate started to protest but Jorge was gone as one of his men brought him a horse. He mounted and his troop were out of the castle gate and galloping across Castle Square, down Broad Street and out of the town.

Kate made her way towards the gate. She needed to get home as it was nearly dusk and soon the town gates would soon be closed. As she got near the gate the guard caught her arm and steered her back into the guardhouse. "Jorge said you're to wait so sit over there and don't think of trying to leave again. You get me in trouble and I won't be pleased. Make Jorge angry and you won't get your reward."

The guard was smirking again and Kate didn't like the way he was looking at her. She sat on the bench and started thinking about what she could tell Will. What reason could she give for not getting back to the farm before nightfall?

"But you don't understand, I have to get back to my husband at our farm. He'll be wondering where I am," Kate pleaded with the guard.

"Jorge said wait, so you wait." He pushed her down onto the bench and left her sitting there.

Darkness fell and Gaspard entered the gatehouse after a very bad day hunting through the woods and along the river. He was cold and wet and he hadn't found any sign of the fugitive at all. He stood by the brazier and looked at the woman sitting on the bench.

"What's she doing here?" he demanded of the guard.

"She came in to tell Jorge she saw your missing messenger and she's waiting for the reward he promised her," answered the guard with a grin and a wink.

Gaspard snorted and went and stood over her.

"Where did you see this man?" asked Gaspard.

"I've told all I know to Jorge," she replied tartly as she was feeling angry about not being allowed to go home.

"And now you can tell me," said Gaspard, making it clear he would not take no for an answer.

Realising she had no option she answered, "I saw a wounded man heading west along the road toward Clun on foot this morning. He was leaning heavily on a stick and he had no pack. I thought it might be the man Jorge described to my husband yesterday when he searched our farm."

"Mmmmm, why didn't your husband come in to report this man?" demanded Gaspard, who was beginning to enjoy himself.

"Because it was me who saw him and therefore I should get the reward. Will only thinks about his precious farm," she replied, trying not to show how nervous Gaspard was making her feel.

"So Jorge has offered a reward, has he? That's interesting. How long ago did he leave?"

"I don't know. Ask the guard, he was here when they left the castle."

Gaspard called the guard over. "When did Jorge leave?"

"Just as it was getting dark but the town gates were still open. It will be hard to find the man tonight in the dark."

Gaspard smiled and it was not a pleasant sight. "Keep her here but put her in a cell." He turned back to Kate. "So your husband hid the messenger from us?"

"No. No, I didn't say that. I just saw the man on the road when I was feeding the sheep," she said, the panic rising in her throat. This was not supposed to be happening. She was supposed to have her reward and be on her way home to show it to Will.

"Do you know what I think?" asked Gaspard. "I think you're lying to me and I think I should chastise you for that."

She didn't understand what he meant but could see the cruelty in his face. He hadn't been able to catch the man who had caused him so much trouble but here was a victim he could torture and by her own confession she would tell him what he wanted to know.

He took her to a cell and chained her to the wall. The guard, unsure of what to do, followed. He started to object and then thought better of it; he had heard of Gaspard's reputation from some of Lord de Grey's men and decided to stay out of the sergeant's business. What was some peasant woman to him?

"Jorge will want her in one piece when he returns," said the guard, trying to distract Gaspard.

"Jorge, he's on a wild goose chase. And this one will tell me what I want to know. I think our messenger is already over the border or maybe even dead. But this one thought she could fool us." Gaspard pushed the guard out of the door. "Go back to your post and stay there."

He closed the door and drew out his dagger. Kate's dress was slit open and it fell away from her body. She started to scream but Gaspard backhanded her across the face. She would have a bruise on her cheek in the morning.

"You'll scream when I'm ready and not before."

The night is going to be a long and pleasant one, the sergeant thought.

Clun

Jorge led his men west at full gallop towards Clun. The road was wider than most tracks in the Marches and they arrived in Clun after the sun had gone down. Jorge rode straight to the castle to request that the castellan turn out his guard and search the town.

The castle stood on its mound above the river with its walled bailey to the west of the town. The keep consisted of the Great Tower with two other towers overlooking the town to the east and the river valley to the west.

The guard smiled as he took Jorge through the bailey to the keep to see the castellan. He knew the castellan would not turn out his men on the whim of a sergeant, no matter who his lord was. They climbed the tower and Jorge was led into the Great Hall at the top of the keep. The castellan was eating his evening meal and seemed in no hurry to listen to this stranger who was intruding on his evening.

The guard went forward and spoke to the castellan who nodded his head and waved Jorge to come forward.

"Who are you and what do you want?" he demanded gruffly as he continued with his meal. He cut some meat and put it in his mouth to chew.

"I am Jorge of Aquitaine, one of Lord de Grey's Sergeants-at-Arms, and I need you to turn out the garrison to help me search for a fugitive who was seen coming this way this morning."

"Lord Reginald de Grey holds no sway here. This is an Arundel castle. If this man is here you will not find him this night; he'll be hidden away by now; have you seen the weather out there? You'll have to wait for the morning."

"But he was seen heading this way this morning. He could get over the border and away. This is very important to Lord de Grey and he will not forget your help," said Jorge, trying to sound as if he wasn't pleading.

"I'm not turning out my men on your whim. So I suppose I'll have to put you up for the night. What's this man done?" the castellan demanded.

"He has some property in his possession that belongs to Lord de Grey."

"So he's a thief. You want me to turn the town upside down for a common thief, at his time of night. If I did that I'd have every tradesman and merchant in the town at my door. No, it will have to wait until morning, that's my final word."

"Can we start at first light?" asked Jorge, now wary of not getting the castellan's cooperation.

"If you're lying to me I'll find out and it'll be your hide I'll have, understand me?" said the castellan. He did not like having another lord's men-at-arms appearing at his castle making demands. He also know knew that if he searched the town he was likely to find nothing and that would not only annoy the townsfolk but also make him look foolish when he did not find what he was looking for. He knew he had to be able to blame Jorge for any disruption caused.

"How do you know this man is in Clun? If he's trying for the border he would avoid any towns and villages. There are plenty of tracks that would lead him past the town through the forest and across the border."

"He's wounded; one of our archers put two arrows into him. I'm surprised he's got this far but he has and Lord de Grey wants him back for questioning. If he wants to travel fast he needs to keep to the easiest route and that's the road via Clun. I think he may have headed for Bishop's Castle or Montgomery to seek help as he is badly wounded."

"So his lordship wants to question a thief?" the castellan mused. *There's more to this than he's saying,* the castellan thought. "I'll not search the town tonight. The townsfolk won't like it and then I'll have trouble on my hands. I have a quiet town here and I don't want it roused. You can watch the roads tomorrow but I doubt you'll find him here. This fugitive, is he Welsh by any chance?"

"I don't know, it's probable. All I know is that his lordship wants him found. We've had men out looking for him for the last two days," complained Jorge.

"I'd heard his lordship is an intemperate man who always gets his own way. I heard he had a number of disagreements and land suits so I suppose he's impatient as well. I pity you and your men out in this weather. Get yourself a cup of wine and have a drink and some food." The castellan turned. "Guard, have the sergeant's men quartered and fed. Tell them they're staying the night."

"Sit down and tell me everything," he said to Jorge. "If you've killed or wounded a Welshman who was not a messenger to whoever then we might have a feud on our hands. And that won't be good for trade and we can expect more raids from over the border. I wish your great lords would keep out of our business in the Marches. We trade with the Welsh but they are not averse to coming over and stealing our stock if we don't deal fairly with them."

Jorge said, "We deal with them in Denbighshire and I know what you mean; his lordship holds land in Wales and he's forever looking for more. I think he'd wipe out the Welsh if he could get away with it."

The castellan took a sip of his wine. He knew he would have to cooperate with Jorge because of Lord de Grey's power but he was not about to damage his own position for no advantage to himself. There were two roads heading west from Clun: one to Bishops Castle and one out to the wilds of the moors. If the fugitive had any sense he would be staying away from any settlements and so the track past the castle would be the road to choose. If the man had any sense he would just travel across country following no roads, just the game tracks through the Clun Forest.

"This man is badly wounded, you say?"

Jorge nodded.

"So how did he get away from the men who shot him if he was so badly wounded?"

"He fell from the top of the hill and the men who shot him did not go down and finish him off. He managed to get across the river Teme and a farmer's wife spotted him on the road to Clun. I only got the news from her late in the afternoon when I returned to Ludlow after a day's searching. So I rode here directly to see if there was any trace of him on the road. The road is a quagmire so there were no tracks that we could see, so we've lost him. We should find him if we search the town because I don't think he could have got much further in his condition."

"So, let me get this right, he was seen heading west. You have no evidence he's actually in Clun?"

"No," Jorge had to admit. He did not like being interrogated and was beginning to lose his patience.

"What time of day did your witness see him?"

"Late morning or early afternoon, she was quite vague. You know how peasants are, they have no method of telling the actual time," said Jorge, even though he did not really know.

"Mmmmm, the more I hear the more you worry me. This man who was shot – you don't know his name, his place of living or in fact anything about him?" asked the castellan rhetorically. He was appalled at the incompetence of Lord de Grey's men. He would have to take measures to distance himself from this man's actions.

Jorge watched the castellan's face. The man was shrewd and Jorge knew he was not going to get much help the morrow. He would set his men to watching the roads out of Clun while he insisted on a search of the town, unpopular as that would be. The castellan was thinking about how he could place any disruption in the town firmly on Jorge's shoulders.

Jorge could see he was in for a long night as the castellan questioned him in detail about the events of the last few days. But he was thankful for being warm and dry, with the added bonus that the castellan's wine was good and plentiful.

"So how does Jorge of Aquitaine wind up in the Welsh borders?"

"My father fought with the English against the French. He moved to England when he was too old to fight any more. I went to Castile with the king's son and after that I wound up here in the Marches with Lord de Grey. I'll tell you this, I've never seen as much rain as falls on this godforsaken country."

"You get used to after a lifetime," said the castellan. "Have you campaigned in Wales?"

"Only as part of the garrison of the Red Castle in Ruthin. We've tried to control the Welsh but they always slip away into the mountains and it's damned hard to follow them. They never just stand and fight."

Ruthin Castle was known as the Red Castle because it was built of red sandstone and stood on a sandstone ridge. Sir Reginald was proud that he had had the gatehouse rebuilt by the king's own builder, Master James of St George. After his improvements the walls were nine feet thick and a hundred feet above the moat. It was a formidable fortress indeed.

"Ah! You have that joy to come then. It's a very different warfare. No pitched battles and few sieges as we Normans hold the castles but the Welsh just disappear into their mountains and to follow them is death. I once followed some Welshmen out into their hills and I lost half my men. They led us up onto a boggy moor and we could see them in the distance but we couldn't find any firm ground to get at them. They just shot my men down and rode away. Not what I expected in a war. They have no honour. Bowmen, peasants all of them."

"I hear Henry of Monmouth is very keen on archers from Cheshire and Wales. And I hear he's keen on any other new war machines his engineers can come up with. He took Welsh archers north to fight the Scots and from what I heard they were some of his best troops."

"It's a bad day when a peasant with a bow can kill a knight in full armour," grumbled the castellan. The wine was having an effect on him.

Jorge had heard many French knights express the same opinion, but he knew the effect of the archers at Crecy and he had seen enough in Aquitaine to know that it was the English and Welsh archers that the French feared, so much so that if they caught an archer they would cut off the index and middle fingers of the archer's right hand to prevent him from using a bow again. The archers would show defiance to the French by waving their two fingers at the knights to show they could shoot a bow.

Jorge took a sip of his wine then he noticed that the castellan had nodded off to sleep. So he took his cloak and stretched out on a bench near the fire and made himself comfortable for the night.

Offa's Dyke

The Welshmen herded the flock of sheep at a steady pace through the night and were over the border before the sun was up. They stopped in the shadow of an old dyke and ate a cold breakfast before continuing on their way into the wild mountains of mid Wales. The rain persisted but at least they were on their own ground.

The leader helped Caradoc from his horse when they reached the Vale of Ceri. They had travelled a few miles out of their way. He was not concerned because it would confuse any pursuers and they would disguise their route once they moved south and away from the border.

"We head south-west from here towards Rhaeadr Gwy," the leader told Caradoc as he passed him his staff. Caradoc took the staff and planted the end firmly onto the ground and used it to steady himself.

"I go north-west towards the Severn," said Caradoc, knowing the leader had told him a lie. The man was just protecting himself and his men.

"Follow the Clun and it will take you up above the Vale of Ceri. You can then drop down off the moor into the Severn Valley. Stick to the forest edge and you can hide if you are followed. Get as deep into the woods as possible; the French believe the woods are haunted and their horses can't ride through such impenetrable forests. Good luck," said the leader as he and his men started driving the sheep away.

Caradoc walked slowly in the direction of his home. He recognised some landmarks so he knew he was getting closer to safety. All he had to do was keep a steady pace and he would make it home. His shoulder was aching badly but his head had cleared. He sat down to rest by a small stream and ate some of the food Will had given him.

He lay down and was soon fast asleep. He woke a few hours later with a red squirrel stealing what was left of his food. He struggled to his feet and shook his cloak to get rid of the crumbs he had spilt. When he leaned over to pick up his staff he felt light-headed and the world began to spin. He grasped he stick and stood straight, taking a deep breath and closing his eyes. He swayed and then planted the staff in the ground to steady himself. He had to get down from the moor and into the vale. Few people travelled so high up so if he collapsed it was unlikely that he would be found.

He did not hear the man come up behind him. The man merged well with the countryside in his clothes – they were the colour of mud, while his cloak was a dull grey colour. The man watched Caradoc as he struggled to keep his balance.

"Where are you headed for?" asked the man suddenly.

Caradoc spun round, lost his balance and fell heavily. Pain coursed through his body; his shoulder was on fire and his head ached. Caradoc lay there as the man stepped forward into the sunlight where Caradoc could see him.

Caradoc groaned as the man leaned over him. He pulled Caradoc's hand away from his wounded shoulder. The man stepped back and considered the boy.

"You didn't answer my question, boy," he said as he watched the younger man writhe in pain on the ground. Caradoc pulled himself into a sitting position and looked up at the man, who had positioned himself with the sun at his back so that Caradoc could not see his face clearly.

With nothing to lose Caradoc said, "The farm south-west of Llanmerwig. If you help me my father will . . ."

"Ah, I know who you are now, your father is Ednyfed ap . . ., well never mind. When I saw you arrive with that herd of sheep I thought you'd been on a raid. Then I saw you falling over. Left you for dead, have they?"

"No, they just helped me over the border. I need to get to my father's farm as soon as possible," explained Caradoc but he did not ask for help due to the man's demeanour.

The man leaned forward and pulled back the bandage. He inspected the wound and stepped back. "That's an arrow wound. Who shot you?"

"I don't know. That's the truth."

"Norman or Saesneg *(English)*, not that it matters; the shape you're in I doubt you'll make it on your own and it's such a short distance."

"Why are you taunting me?"

"Because it's fun," the man snapped back. "Only kidding. Where were the sheep being herded to?" he asked.

"They said they were going to Rhaeadr Gwy," said Caradoc, knowing he was not giving away any secret.

"That was too easy," said the man almost to himself.

"That's what they told me, but they might have lied."

The man threw back his head and laughed. Caradoc watched him, not seeing what was funny. Eventually the man stopped laughing and picked up Caradoc's staff.

"Well I suppose we'd better get you home then. They call me Gwyn Mochyn and I'll tell you how I got the name as we march you home."

They started walking, slowly at first and then with a little more rhythm. Where the pain had held him back he now used it to drive himself on. Just a few more miles but the terrain was tough and the ground underfoot was very wet and it sapped the legs of energy. Caradoc found he had to take regular stops to rest, even though Gwyn Mochyn set a very easy pace and supported Caradoc as he walked. They usually stopped where Gwyn could find some water to drink but he made Caradoc drink sparingly, not wanting the boy to overload his already weakened body.

It was nearly mid-afternoon when they arrived at the top of the Vastre and they looked down on the small market town of Llanfair yng Nghedewain (Newtown). Further down the valley was Ednyfed's home. It was just a mile down the hillside but the distance seemed much further. Caradoc set off, keeping himself hidden from the main track by following the woods and hedges that covered the slopes. Gwyn followed a yard behind the boy.

Although the farm was so close Gwyn made Caradoc sit and rest. He took some bread and cheese from his pack and split it with Caradoc. As the boy started to eat, Gwyn said, "Well I'd better tell you the story of how I got my name before we meet someone on the road and they give you the wrong version."

"We were raiding across the border further north near Oswestry where the Saxon king was killed in battle. We were after cattle, of course; they travel faster than pigs or sheep and we wanted a quick raid. In and out. That lot you were with were travelling very slow; I was able to keep up on foot and I only picked up your trail from just north of Clun."

Caradoc listened as Gwyn droned on. The food did him good but when he started to get up Gwyn pushed him back down.

"Rest or you won't make it," said the woodsman.

"But it's just down there," said Caradoc, indicating with his arm.

"It's still two miles and I'll get you there once you've heard my story."

Caradoc lay back on the grass and stared up at the sky as Gwyn continued his story.

"We were across the border and we found the herd of cattle where we knew it would be, but there were also a number of pigs. In particular there was a small suckling pig which I thought would be good for the summer feast."

Gwyn continued, "Well, we got the herd started and while the others were moving the cattle I went and caught the pig. I picked it up and put it across my saddle. As we were driving the cattle west the piglet started to squeal. The farmer heard it and came out with his sons and chased after us. We escaped but we couldn't keep the cattle together so the only thing we got from the raid was that noisy pig. So they called me Gwyn Mochyn because of that damn suckling pig."

Caradoc smiled at the story but didn't make a comment. Gwyn pulled him to his feet. "You're not going to make it, are you?"

Gwyn leaned forward and lifted Caradoc across his broad shoulders and set off at a slow pace over the hill. Gwyn walked slowly, trying not to jar Caradoc as he walked down the sloping fields towards the farm.

It took Gwyn over an hour to travel the short distance to the farm and he was wary of just walking into the farmyard with the wounded boy in case Ednyfed thought that he had wounded the boy.

When they reached the farmyard Gwyn lowered Caradoc to the ground and then the boy called out his father's name, "Ednyfed. Ednyfed."

Ednyfed and Owain came out of the house when they heard his call. Ednyfed had a sword in his hand and Owain, Caradoc's brother, was carrying an axe. Caradoc's mother came from the kitchen and was appalled when she saw what state her son was in. His younger brother, Owain, picked him up and carried him into the house. Owain laid Caradoc on the table and their mother removed the poultice and started to clean the wound. She stripped away his clothes, dropping them on the hard-packed earthen floor, and washed away the blood and bile. More puss was cleaned out of the wound and she bathed it with an infusion of honey and herbs. When she was finished she applied a fresh poultice to draw any more splinters from the wound.

Ednyfed looked with some askance at Gwyn Mochyn. "I found him on the other side of the vale and I carried him here. It wasn't me who shot him. If it had been he'd be dead."

"Then who did?" Ednyfed asked, watching Gwyn with distrust.

"He says he doesn't know. He was shot on the other side of the border. I saw him after he was dropped off by some sheep herders who were heading south-west. If what he told me is true then I doubt they can tell you more than where they picked him up. I followed them from this side of Clun."

Ednyfed nodded and Gwyn Mochyn moved away. He did not turn his back on the farm until he was a good five hundred yards from the farmyard because he knew what a good archer could do with a bow and he knew that both Ednyfed and Owain were good archers. Once he was away from the farm he wondered how he could take advantage of the knowledge he had just acquired. Surely Lord Rhys ap Hywel would like to know about a young man being shot on his way home through the Marches. So he set off for the market town in the valley to find the Welsh lord.

Ednyfed, Caradoc's father, rode to Ceri to see if anybody had been following Caradoc and Gwyn Mochyn. He asked anyone he passed if they had seen the boy or any strangers in the area. No one he met had seen anyone. So he told them to let him know if anyone asked for a wounded boy. He also asked about Gwyn Mochyn and though most of the farmers in the area laughed about keeping their pigs locked up if he was about, though none would accuse him of trying to kill a boy.

When Ednyfed returned, Owain pointed to the wound and said, "That's an arrow wound from a bodkin. This was no hunting accident. The arrowhead is English; I bought some like it in Shrewsbury last month."

"That proves nothing then," said the older man.

Ednyfed sat down next to Caradoc and asked him to tell them what had happened but his mother shooed him away.

Caradoc was fed some broth by his mother and then she made him lie down and rest. His father and brother wanted him to tell them the full story of what had happened to him, but he drifted in to sleep and then woke to find them still waiting to hear what had happened.

Slowly he told them of his visit to Oxford and of the city. He told his mother about his uncle Geraint who was a monk and how he was working in the scriptorium copying books onto vellum. He told them how his uncle had shown him how to use a pen and how they decorated the pages. He told them of the Welsh bard who came singing songs of sedition around the colleges and how many Welsh scholars and tradesmen had packed up and headed back to Wales. "There is something going on with the marcher lords and the king but I don't know what. Uncle Geraint said I should leave after he heard one of the bards singing outside the abbey."

Ednyfed's patience was sorely tried as he wanted to know more about how Caradoc had been shot and wounded, but he held his tongue until the boy finished telling his mother about Geraint, her beloved brother. Eventually Caradoc told his father about his journey home. He told of his walk through the country and how he had visited Clee hill to look out over the Shropshire countryside. That was why he had been on the ridge north of Ludlow when he was shot.

Caradoc explained where he had hidden his pack on the escarpment above the Teme. He described where he was standing on the ridge, looking for a route down to the river. His description of how he had been shot from behind by two archers angered his father so much that he got up and punched the wall with his fist, causing the wattle to crumble. Owain, who was leaning on the wall, just listened to the unfolding story.

"I don't understand it, why would Lord Grey want me dead? I don't even know him. It was his man Gaspard who either shot me himself or had me shot. From what I overheard the horsemen say they are looking for a messenger. But I am carrying no messages except from Uncle Geraint to Mam."

"If you weren't wearing a pack they could have mistaken you for a messenger but that's no reason to kill you," said his brother Owain who had listened to his brother's story. Owain was not a man who showed his emotions.

"Where's your bow?" asked his father Ednyfed.

"I lost it in the fall and I lost my arrow bag when I landed. It helped break my fall," explained Caradoc.

"Tell me more about the farmer who helped you."

"His name is Will. The farm was three or four miles west from where I was shot, this side of the river Teme. He could have given me up when Jorge, Lord Grey's man, was there but he took me in and that poultice was done by his wife. His name is Will but I didn't hear his wife's name."

Ednyfed looked at his son and how badly he was hurt and made a decision. "Owain, go and tell my brothers I think we need to pay a little visit over the border to collect Caradoc's pack. We need to do it quickly because if we don't they will think they can attack us with impunity. Make sure every man has a horse and keep an eye out for that rogue Gwyn Mochyn. I know he brought Caradoc home but I still don't trust him."

His wife, Mags, was not happy but she did not try to dissuade her husband as she knew his mind was made up. Caradoc was the victim of an unprovoked attack and if nothing was done about it the English would continue to take advantage. A raid over the border to collect Caradoc's pack and to relieve the English of some compensation was what Ednyfed intended. He would also visit the farmer to see if he could tell him more about why Lord Grey wanted to kill Caradoc.

Once Caradoc had eaten his broth she sent him off to his bed. He was asleep as soon as his head touched the pillow. Mags sat and watched his chest rise and fall as he breathed, and she thought about how she had nearly lost her eldest son. She sat there until her daughter Carys called her when the evening meal was ready.

It was evening when Owain returned. He had spoken to various members of the family and the message had gone out about a raid over the border. By morning the whole of Powys would know Caradoc had been attacked and wounded for no good reason.

There were many Welshmen who had a grudge against their English neighbours who would gladly join a raid over the border. The 1284 Statute of Wales was the first of many anti-Welsh laws which the English enforced to try and wrest control of the principality from its native people. There were many injustices and the Marches were ready for a backlash against the rule of the arrogant marcher lords.

Ednyfed would select the men he wanted to take with him. He wanted a raiding party not an invasion which really would provoke the English into retaliation. He did not want to raise such a fuss that he drew the attention of the king or his young son Henry of Monmouth who was making such an impression as Prince of Wales. He knew he could not challenge the power of the English and their castles such as the great fortress at Ludlow.

Vale of Ceri

Ednyfed's brother Huw was the first to arrive. He was a large man and he carried a six-foot bow and a large axe. "I hear you're going to hunt an Englishman or two."

The bow was only four inches shorter than the man, whose red hair made him stand out like a beacon. He was not just tall, he had a huge chest and his shoulders showed that he had the strength to pull the longbow he carried so lightly. Huw was a giant of a man. The weapons looked like toys in the hands of such a large man.

"Do you want to see Caradoc? Or do you just want pick to fight with the English?" scolded Mags, but Huw just grinned at her.

"How is the boy?"

"He's badly wounded and running a fever and the journey from Ludlow took a lot out of him. He's very, very weak; they nearly killed him. If the arrow had been a little further to the right he would be dead. It's lucky Gwyn Mochyn found him and carried him here."

"Gwyn Mochyn? I thought he was only good for stealing pigs. I'll just go up and cheer him up with some stories of what we'll do to those English swine," said Huw with a huge smile that split his face. "Gwyn Mochyn, who would believe it?"

"You'll do no such thing, he's sleeping. The arrow went right through his shoulder, he's got a high fever and he still managed to walk home. I'll not have you, you great lump, disturbing him." Mags said as she pushed him towards the kitchen.

"The lad is tougher than he looks, isn't he," said Huw with a wide grin and Mags hit him hard on the shoulder. "Do you really think he'll make a monk like Geraint?"

"You big ox, they could have killed my Caradoc," she said angrily, annoyed at Huw's insensitivity. "And why would he make a good monk like Geraint?"

"No reason but all that praying. It's because he survived. That's why we have to teach them a lesson. We can't let them get away with shooting the lad, can we?"

"Just so long as you don't get killed teaching them a lesson, you big lump." She turned her back on him and left him standing in the yard outside the kitchen door.

As they day went on other men arrived and the family started to prepare a plan of action. It was noon when Tegwyn, Lord Rhys's knight, arrived to see what Ednyfed was planning. He was quite surprised when he saw the number of men preparing to go on the raid across the border. He dismounted and went to the house to talk to Ednyfed.

"Is there no other way of dealing with this?" Tegwyn asked. "The English will know who is raiding and why. Just having all these men here constitutes breaking the law."

"It's only an English law and therefore it doesn't apply here. We're not English. We're Welsh. The boy was just travelling home from his uncle's monastery in Oxford; he was doing no harm to anyone and they shot him in the back with no provocation. Do you want to see his wounds?" Ednyfed asked. When Tegwyn did not reply he continued, "Then they hunted him as if it was open season on Welshmen. How often do we have to put up with this before we do something about it? I know our Welsh lords won't do anything so it's left to us. Your Lord Rhys has his licence from the king so what does he care? So we'll just take a little trip to collect Caradoc's pack."

"To collect his pack, and that's it, is it? Just remember who you owe allegiance to." Sir Tegwyn knew he had said the wrong thing as soon as he said it. To threaten a man like Ednyfed was to challenge him and he would not let that go until he had satisfaction.

Ednyfed ignored the threat and pointed out of the doorway. "Tell that to them. When we go over the border they treat us like the dirt on their shoes and now they are trying to come here and take our lands. No Welshman can own land – you remember the law, their Statute of Wales in '84 when their parliament passed a law with no reference to us, the people of Wales. They've tried to kill my son and all you can do is worry about what your Lord Rhys will say." Ednyfed pulled a face and continued. "Well you can tell him that from me, if you've the guts," Ednyfed said, showing how angry he was. "Tell him if he'd stood up to the English we'd have supported him but he appeased them and now we are reaping the rewards of his failure."

Tegwyn was taken aback. He had not expected this depth of feeling of injustice and hostility from Ednyfed. He knew he would say nothing to Lord Rhys and he also knew that Lord Rhys would take no action. Tegwyn knew Lord Rhys had worked hard to keep the peace in this part of Wales, not just for himself but for everyone. War benefited no one. Tegwyn knew Lord Rhys was too preoccupied with holding onto his own position with the English king and the other marcher magnates to stop them from just raping the principality of its manpower and resources.

Just as he thought Ednyfed had finished, Ednyfed said pointedly, "If I remember correctly you lost your lands in Brecon to the Earl of Lancaster, did you not? He's now the king." Ednyfed emphasised the point that Henry, the Duke of Lancaster, was now Henry IV and that he had treated the Welsh very badly in the lands he held around Brecon before he became king.

Tegwyn shuddered at the memory and the loss of face he had suffered at the hands of the duke. He said nothing and retreated to the yard. *The Duke of Lancaster has since become King Henry IV,* he thought. It was the loss of his lands to the duke which had had made him go into the service of Lord Rhys, and he knew he had little chance of regaining his lost property while Henry remained king. The memory brought back the bitterness he felt towards the English king and he resolved to do anything he could to take his revenge on the English. Tegwyn called one of his men to him. "Paul, go with these men and report back to me everything that happens. Make sure you are able to escape if they get involved in a fight or skirmish so you can report back to me. Do you understand?"

"I was talking to Huw, this will be a quick raid not a full chevauchee; it will be in and out, fast. These men have been doing this for centuries. They don't fight pitched battles, they hit and run. By the time the English know they have been hit, the raiding party will be miles away and back over the border," said Paul as he watched the men preparing to ride.

"Just make sure *you* don't get caught," Tegwyn nodded and went to his horse, mounted and rode away. There was nothing more he could do for now. He would ride to his lord's court and report to him what had happened to young Caradoc ap Ednyfed and the repercussions that were about to take place.

Tegwyn knew that the raid was ill-advised but he could not prevent it and the best he could do was to have Lord Rhys distance himself from the raiders by being in Shrewsbury with either the Talbots or with Sir Edmund Mortimer at Wigmore Castle or even with Lancaster's relatives in Ludlow.

Tegwyn led his men out of Ednyfed's farmyard and out to the main track between the town in the valley and the Vale of Ceri. As they reached the end of the lane that led to Ednyfed's farm he spotted a man hiding behind a hedge waiting for him to pass. The man he recognised as Ifor ap Goronwy, the local bowyer and fletcher, obviously bringing supplies for the raid. Tegwyn made a note but just rode on by.

Ifor waited for a few minutes, then he guided his pack horses down the lane to the farm. He was welcomed by Huw and Owain who guided him into the barn, undercover and out of sight.

Ifor laid out a selection of bows with differing draw strengths. He had wicker baskets with sheaves of arrows; each basket's arrowheads had a different purpose. He also had a selection of arrow heads and bowstrings, and even some resin to keep the bows in their best condition.

While he was setting out his stall, Huw and Owain set up a butt, made of wood and straw, in the field below the farm. Ifor waved to them that he was ready and they walked back to look at the bows he had brought with him.

"Edwin the smith will be here as soon as he can get away. He's got some swords, falchions, axes and spears. I think he said he even has a few coats of mail," Ifor informed them.

Huw laughed and said, "We're going on a raid not a full scale war, I don't think we'll need the armour."

"He'll probably have some brigandines as well; they are lighter but they give good protection."

Owain was looking at the bows with great interest. Ifor noticed and asked, "What strength are you looking for?"

"My bow pull's about a hundred and twenty pounds but I think I can pull more. I've had that old bow for two years now and I think I need a new one. This was Caradoc's old one, so it's had some good use."

Ifor steered the young man towards some six-foot bow staves at the end of his stall. He picked two up. "This one's ash and it has a hundred and thirty pound pull. And this yew is more powerful again; it has a hundred and seventy pound pull. Why don't you try them? I thought Huw could try the yew."

"What do you think, Huw?" asked Owain as he picked up the bows.

"The only way to know is to string the bow and shoot it," said his uncle.

Owain turned to Ifor who produced two bow strings and handed them to Owain. "Try them out."

Ifor split a sheaf of hunting arrows and passed them to Owain. "Those are for hunting, most of the others are cloth yard bodkins," he said, referring to the armour piercing arrowheads which he had tipped the arrows with.

Huw and Owain strung the bows and went to the field to test them. Owain shot his own bow first then the ash bow, which sent the arrow slashing into the butt of straw they had set up as a target. The arrow sank much deeper into the target but it was the yew bow that made the greatest impression. Owain knocked his arrow. Drew the bow and he could feel the strain across his chest. The arrow flew and stuck the butt with such power that the arrow exited from the rear side of the straw target.

Huw took the bow and gave it a test draw and then nocked an arrow. He drew the bow, shot and hit the target dead centre with the arrow going straight through the target and out the other side. The arrow skimmed along the ground and finally came to rest sticking into a mole hill.

"I'd take the yew if I was you. The other one is good but the yew gives you much more penetration. You'll soon grow strong enough to pull it like me," said Huw, handing the bow to Owain.

Ednyfed was watching them shoot from the gate of the field when Edwin the smith arrived in the farmyard. Edwin's horses were laden with arms concealed in rolls of cloth. He smiled at Ifor and said, "I was not sure what to bring so I brought it all."

Ednyfed left his post and ushered Edwin into the barn. Ifor and Ednyfed helped Edwin unload his horses. They set up a grinding wheel for the men to sharpen their weapons. Edwin and Ifor put the smith's weapons and armour on display. He hung up two coats of mail and a dozen brigandines, a defensive jacket of metal plates on cloth. He also had jupons in various sizes, short leather jackets worn over chain mail. He laid out some pourpoints, quilted doublets and bassinets in several sizes. He hung several jacks on the dividing stalls of the barn. The jacks were defensive leather coats, with several layers reinforced with metal studs or plates.

Once the defensive garments were displayed he laid out a tarpaulin on the floor and placed his display of edged weapons on it. He had swords, falchions, poniards and bollock daggers. He produced several poleaxes with their axe and hammer heads and a morning star. Last, he drew several misercordes, the mercy daggers used to despatch wounded enemies and even a kledyv, an ancient Welsh short sword of about two feet in length.

Some of the other men wandered in to look at the weapons. Some men tried the swords for balance. One man picked up a poleaxe and started waving it about.

Edwin picked up a poleaxe and gave them a demonstration of how it should be used. Ednyfed was impressed by the older man's prowess with the weapon.

"I wasn't always a smith, I did some campaigning too," said Edwin as he caught his breath after his exertions.

Ednyfed picked up the poleaxe and went through some of the exercises Edwin had but he was not as fluent as the older man. He handed back the weapon and looked round at the men who had been watching.

"What are you intending to do?" asked Edwin as he laid the poleaxe back with the others on display.

"Initially collect Caradoc's pack and his bow if we can find them. If we can I want to talk to the farmer who helped him and if we can capture one of his pursuers then maybe we will find out what this is all about. About these?" Ednyfed waved his arm over the weapons on display.

"You mean payment?" asked Edwin.

"I do," said Ednyfed, knowing that most of the men had no coin to purchase what was on offer.

"It depends on who needs what. If you are going to bring back some booty from the raid, I can wait for payment. If it's chain mail or something that can be identified, then it will either have to be cash or kind."

Ifor chipped in, "I'll let you have the arrows for a share of what the raid produces. Bows will have to be individually agreed, they're worth much more."

Ednyfed inspected the arrows split them between hunting arrows and bodkin or war arrows. He told each man what the cost of the arrows and Ifor noted who had taken arrows and of which kind they were. He made a list on a piece of parchment and each man made his mark.

Iolo looked at the edged weapons and asked, "How much for the kledyv?"

"Five nobles," said Edwin as he picked up the old sword.

Iolo searched his pouch and said, "I couldn't go more than two."

"I couldn't let it go for less than four nobles," said the smith, knowing from the look on Iolo's face that the man really wanted the old weapon. Edwin knew Iolo had recognised what it for what it was.

"Three nobles and I'm done," said Iolo as he checked his pouch again.

"What else have you got?" asked Edwin.

"Just a few sols I won at dice."

"How many?" Edwin persisted.

Iolo counted the shards of metal in his hand. "Nine."

"It's yours for three nobles and five sols, and that's my last word," said Edwin holding out his hand..

Iolo shook the offered hand clinching the deal and then passed over the coins and picked up the ancient weapon and took it to roll into his blankets.

Several other man tried weapons and one or two purchases were made.

Owain came back to the barn with Huw following. He placed the two bows back with others Ifor had on display.

"What did you think?" asked the bowyer.

"The ash is good but I really like the yew, it's got that extra bit of power to penetrate a target. It's a special bow," said Owain with enthusiasm.

"I thought Huw would be the only one who would be able to draw the yew. That's why I brought it up," explained Ifor as he picked up the bow.

Huw chuckled, "The boy can draw it fine and the more practice he has the better and stronger he'll be."

Ifor could smell a sale and looked at Ednyfed, knowing that the boy didn't have the money for the bow. Ednyfed picked up the bow, strung it and, taking a few arrows, headed for the field where the butt was waiting. He stopped a hundred paces from the butt and stuck the arrows into the ground so they could be plucked easily. He nocked an arrow and shot. As the first arrow was in the air he picked a second, nocked it and shot. He continued until he ran out of arrows. On the last arrow he drew the bow as far back as he could mange and let fly. The arrow flew through the air, straight through the target and into the ground behind it.

Ednyfed walked towards the butt followed by Ifor and the rest of the men. They inspected the target to see the damage the arrows had done. Ednyfed turned to Owain and said, "Get that old helmet from the barn and bring me a bodkin arrow."

When Owain returned he placed the old metal helmet on the target, suspending it from a piece of twine. Ednyfed took the bodkin arrow and marched back a hundred paces. He nocked the arrow and took careful aim. He released the arrow and it hit the helmet, going through the front plate of metal. The tip of the bodkin sank deeply into the back of the helmet with the tip sticking into the wood of the butt. The impact of the arrow toppled the butt over.

Ifor was the first to inspect the helmet. Owain joined him. "I told you it was a good bow."

Ednyfed arrived and inspected his handiwork. "Almost through two layers of metal," said Ifor. The men gathered round to look at it as Ednyfed hung the helmet back on the butt.

He turned to Owain and said, "Repeat that and the bow is yours."

Owain ran back to the barn to get another bodkin arrow. When he returned Ednyfed was waiting for him at the spot from where he had fired his arrow. He handed Owain the bow and the boy nocked his arrow.

Owain took a deep breath and drew the bow, aimed and released. The arrow flew true and slammed into the helmet. Ednyfed and Owain walked the hundred paces to the butt and inspected it. The arrow had gone through both sides of the helmet and buried its head into the butt. A feat for a seasoned archer let alone a youngster.

"Looks like you have yourself a new bow," said Ednyfed. He left Owain standing there and walked off, taking Ifor by the elbow to guide him back to the barn to haggle about the price.

Huw laughed and punched Owain in the arm. "You'd better get practising so that bow becomes an extension of your arm."

Owain took another arrow and did just that.

Kerry – Clun – Welsh Marches

Ednyfed formed the men into two groups. One group, with Ednyfed at its head, would ride to collect Caradoc's pack from the escarpment near Ludlow. On the way they would visit Clun to glean any information they could get from friends in the border town. They could then lay waste the countryside as they returned, knowing who to strike and who to leave be.

The second smaller group would go to Offa's Dyke on the moors and set up a defensive camp to wait for the returning raiders with fresh horses. They would wait until the castellan of Clun sent his men out after the main group and then they would raid the farms around Clun. This would create a diversion for the first party coming back from Ludlow.

Huw, who was leading the second party, would let it be known in Clun why the raids were happening. They would stir up the local farmers and peasants which would make the Mortimers very unhappy. The Earls of March had ruled the Marches with a heavy hand for many years, almost from the time of William the Bastard.

None of the raiders noticed a horseman following them at a distance but none would have been surprised if he had joined them. He was a man of uncertain allegiance.

———

Leaving his men in a clearing in the Clun Forest, Ednyfed rode with Owain to Clun where they were met on the road entering the town by some of Jorge's men who were searching and questioning everyone who was entering or leaving the town.

"What's your business here?" demanded the man-at-arms in Lord de Grey's livery.

Owain translated for his father, although Ednyfed had a reasonably grasp of the language.

"What business is it of theirs?" asked Ednyfed gruffly in Welsh to Owain who gave a more diplomatic reply.

"Lord de Grey's business," the man-at-arms insisted after Owain translated.

"We're here to collect payment of a debt," said Owain in English and the men-at-arms let them through as they were obviously not the messenger they were looking for. The two men rode to the inn of the Raven on the eastern edge of town. There they entered the inn and asked to speak to the landlord.

Glyn, the landlord, poured them tankards of ale and waved them to move to the end of the bar away from his other customers. "I don't see you over here very often."

"In Welsh," muttered Owain as he put coin on the bar for the drinks.

"Why are Lord de Grey's men guarding the town?" asked Ednyfed, having recognised Grey's insignia on their uniforms.

"They're searching for a wounded man so the rumour goes," said Glyn. "They've already searched the town, and they are now searching the farms nearby. I don't think they really know what to do as this messenger seems to have dropped out of sight. The sooner they find him, the better. It's bad for business."

"How many of Grey's men are there?"

"Why do you want to know?" asked Glyn, his curiosity getting the better of him.

"What's this man they are looking for done?" asked Owain, answering a question with a question.

"He's a thief, according to the castellan. He has something belonging to Lord de Grey and he wants it back, at least that's the story." Glyn poured himself a drink and took a sip.

Owain looked at his father. The older man asked again, "How many of Lord de Grey's men are there?"

"About ten. They've been in here twice because they know I'm Welsh," said Glyn with some resentment. "And that makes me a suspect. They made threats and then they even tried to offer me a bribe, but I don't know anything."

Ednyfed smiled as an idea formulated in his mind; it was not a pleasant smile. "I wonder, would you do me a favour?"

Glyn read the look on Ednyfed face and became very apprehensive. "What did you have in mind?"

"Find the leader of Lord Grey's men and tell them that a customer mentioned that he saw a man walking with the aid of a stick. He was walking westward on the other side of Black Hill. Tell him that your customer said the man looked in a bad way, and that he fell down and struggled to get up like he was badly wounded."

"I don't want to get into trouble with the castellan; he's made it very clear that I'm only here on sufferance. He'll clear me out if he can; he's been looking for an excuse since he was appointed. You know the laws about a Welshman owning property and I could lose all I have."

"Well here's a chance for you to get into his good favour. I don't think he really wants Grey's men in his town any more than you do." Ednyfed continued, "Go to the castellan and tell him about the wounded man seen at Black Hill, let him pass it on to Grey's man and that will prove your loyalty to the castellan. And I'm sure he wants to be rid of Grey's men as much as the rest of the townsfolk. Give us two hours and then go to the castle to tell your story."

"What will be said over the border if I do this?" asked Glyn, concerned about his reputation. He did not want to be seen as an English informer even though he lived in England. Much of Glyn's income came from travelling Welshmen who wanted a friendly place to stay and refresh themselves. Becoming an informer could lose him a good portion of his trade.

Ednyfed smiled reassuringly. "We'll make it known how helpful you are to the right people. This will work for both of us and we can guide more business in your direction. And you gain the gratitude of the castellan."

Glyn recognised what Ednyfed was saying and the implications behind it. This could make his business much more profitable if he became a staging point for his fellow countrymen, especially the sort of men Ednyfed was talking about. It would also help to keep the castellan off his back.

"I'll do it, but I suggest you leave now. I have to deal with my other customers before I can go to the castle."

Glyn picked up his tankard and went back down the bar to serve another customer. Owain and Ednyfed finished their beers and left.

Clun

Glyn waited for a full two hours and then he made his way through the town to the castle. At the gatehouse he was kept waiting by the guard until the castellan came down to see how Jorge's searches were progressing. The castellan asked the guard why Glyn was waiting at the gatehouse and the guard just shrugged.

He beckoned Glyn to come to him and demanded, "What do you want?"

"I have some information that might be useful to you, sir," said the Welshman in a quite voice.

"Well spit it out," said the castellan impatiently.

"A customer said he saw a wounded man on the other side of Black Hill this morning. I wondered if it might be the man you are looking for?" said Glyn, keeping all emotion from his face.

The castellan hit Glyn hard across the face. "Why have you taken so long to come and tell me?" he raged at the dumbfounded Welshman.

Glyn staggered back against the wall. He pulled himself back to his full height and looked down at the castellan. He resisted the urge to leap forward and beat the man senseless, remembering what Ednyfed had said. He took a deep breath to calm himself. *I'll have my sweet revenge for this insult later,* he thought.

"I overheard him about an hour ago and came here directly. This man kept me here waiting," said Glyn indicating to the guard. "I suggest you hit him not me. Why should I bother to try to help you when I'm treated thus?"

The castellan ignored Glyn's comment and turned to the guard.

"Go and find Jorge and tell him to come to me, now!" the castellan ordered the guard. The guard ran off toward the road to Montgomery.

Glyn started to walk away.

"Stop! You'd better come with me and tell me everything you know." The castellan was sorry he had hit Glyn but could not bring himself to apologise to him. Glyn wiped his hand over his face and followed the castellan into the guardhouse and told him what he had supposedly overheard.

Jorge arrived with some of his men and demanded to know what knowledge Glyn had about the wounded man. Glyn patiently repeated his story and Jorge pressed him for details he didn't have. Men were sent to Glyn's tavern to arrest the traveller but there was no one there when they got there.

"I think you had better go and investigate this sighting, don't you?" said the castellan, hoping to see the back of Jorge and his men.

"Do you trust this man?" asked Jorge pointedly to the castellan.

"He has never lied to me before, I don't see why he should do so now," replied the castellan, not lying but not exactly telling the truth. "I think you must have ridden past your fugitive in the dark. It makes sense, especially if he was wounded and on foot and you were a horseback. A wounded man on foot could not travel as fast as you and your men on horseback."

"We'll be back if this is a wild goose chase," Jorge stared directly at Glyn, "and you'll be the first one I'll come to see."

Glyn protested, "I wish I hadn't bothered to tell you if this is all the thanks I get." With that he turned and walked out of the guardroom. Outside, he smiled to himself as he walked back to his inn.

The castellan watched the publican go and he turned to Jorge. "If you keep insulting my people they will not bother to try and help you in future. He'll tell all the other traders how you've treated him and they are already displeased with the arrogant way you have dealt with them," said the castellan, who was rather pleased with the outcome.

Jorge summoned the rest of his men and they swiftly saddled their horses and left to search the eastern road towards Ludlow.

The castellan watched as Jorge led his troop down the road, hoping that they would not return. Glyn had done him a favour and the Welshman may be useful in the future. He would go and have a quiet chat with him when there were no prying eyes to observe him. A Welsh informer could be very useful and the man had actually rid him of Lord de Grey's man, even if it was only for a day. He would like to make sure that Jorge would not return but he would have to leave that to fate.

The castellan called the guard over and said, "If that publican comes again, bring him directly to me. Do you understand?"

"What about the sergeant's orders?" asked the guard.

"I said, TO ME, you dolt, understand? I'll let the sergeant know and all the guards are to do the same. And treat him with respect but make sure as few of the townspeople notice as possible."

"Yes sir," said the guard, surprised at the castellan's sudden change of attitude towards Glyn.

The castellan smiled to himself and went into the castle to get his men back into barracks so he could prepare them if something went wrong. He sent out a sergeant to gather all his men back at the gatehouse to be ready if Jorge returned. He did not care about Jorge but he was worried about Lord de Grey. If he should arrive then he could have a problem but then a thought went through his mind, *Why should he worry?*

After all, he already had his scapegoat.

Nobody noticed a single horseman lead his horse out onto the Ludlow road. He mounted and followed the troop at a leisurely pace.

Black Hill, East of Clun

Ednyfed sent Owain to collect all their men from Offa's Dyke and Clun Forest to bring them to Black Hill. Ednyfed rode to the small valley on the eastern side of the hill. He had a short time to set his ambush and he was going to make sure his plan would work. First, he surveyed the valley on his horse, riding along the tree line looking for places where his men could conceal themselves. He purposely did not ride up the centre of the valley because he wanted no horse tracks there when Lord de Grey's men arrived. The only track there would be of a wounded man. He wanted to make sure that he would lose no men in this ambush.

There was a small stream flowing down the centre of the valley and the slopes of the hill were covered in leafy trees with plenty of undergrowth. All he had to do was lure Lord de Grey's men up the centre of the valley to where his men could cut them down with their longbows. He cut a staff and used it to set a trail a blind man could follow up the southern side of the stream. He dug the staff into the ground to make an easy trail to follow and also so that it would seem as if the traveller was badly wounded and needed the staff to keep him on his feet.

By the time Owain and Huw arrived he had the plan perfected. Ednyfed directed the men to hide their horses on the south-western side of Black Hill near to Pen-y-wern. He split his men into three groups. One group he sent to the southern slope and the second to the northern slope of the valley.

The men were told to hide in the trees and wait for Owain's signal. Owain was to play the part of his wounded brother in the centre of the valley. He would take up his position at the upper end of the valley, and would appear if the riders did not follow the tracks Ednyfed had laid to entice them. The third group was led by Ednyfed and they went to the south-eastern end of the forest looking back up the valley. Three of them kept their horses and rode round the track to a small clearing to wait so that Lord de Grey's men would not hear the horses when they arrived.

Ednyfed had the men eat and told them to string their bows in readiness. He told them that it would be best if no Englishmen survived the ambush. The men nodded in agreement. "However, I want their leader alive until I have spoken to him. Shoot the men and only shoot the horses if you really have to, I want to take as many of their horses back with us," he commanded. "We might as well make some profit out of this raid."

Owain went to his position at the centre of the small vale. He waved to the men and they all made sure they could see him. He moved back into the trees out of sight and sat down at the base of a tree. He took some bread and mutton from his pouch and started to eat.

They waited for the English to arrive. As ever this was the hard part of any raid, the waiting for the action to start. Time moved slowly.

They waited just over an hour for Lord de Grey's men to enter the funnel of the valley. Ednyfed sent a runner to alert his horsemen and all of his men hidden in the trees notched arrows to their bows.

The lead rider dismounted and pointed out the stick marks Ednyfed had made with his staff. The man mounted again and rode forward following the tracks. The rest of the men followed, spread out in a skirmish line. They did not take the normal precautions a patrol would in enemy country. After all, they were chasing a severely wounded man who from the tracks was at the edge of his reserves. They followed the tracks straight into the valley following the stream. Owain watched as they got closer to his position. He aimed his new bow at the lead rider. The more the distance decreased, the more sure Owain became as the rider came within fifty yards. *Wait until he's really close.*

The rest of the Welshmen were now in the shadows of the tree line, waiting to fire their retribution into the English horsemen.

At twenty-five yards Owain couldn't miss and he stepped away from the tree and loosed his first arrow into the lead rider's face. The arrow went straight through his cheek and into the man's brain. He was dead before he hit the ground. Owain's second arrow took the larger man who was riding just behind the tracker in the shoulder, turning him in the saddle.

The rest of the Welshmen were now pouring arrows into the flanks of the patrol from both sides of the valley. Men and horses went down as the arrows hit home.

Jorge tried to turn his horse but the valley was sealed off by the Welsh horsemen. There was no escape. Arrows fell from both sides until all of Lord de Grey's men were down and wounded at least once. With his tracker dead, and most of his men down, Jorge was angry that he had walked so stupidly into an ambush. *Whoever planned this trap knew what he was doing*, thought Jorge.

The Welshmen moved in and finished off any wounded with their falchions and daggers. The only man left alive was Jorge, and he was wounded in three places. He tried to turn his horse to escape but each time he was shot with another arrow. The archers were careful to shoot him in non-vital areas of his body.

Owain ran forward and hit Jorge's horse with a huge blow to his muzzle and the horse collapsed, throwing his rider to the ground. The Welsh horsemen rounded up the horses and herded them into a meadow by the stream where the frightened horses began to graze.

Ednyfed walked forward and stood over the prone form of the sergeant. "I hear you're hunting Welshmen?" he said almost casually.

Jorge snarled, "Just wait until Lord de Grey hears of this."

"What makes you think he ever will?" Ednyfed swung his arm in a circle. "They're all dead and you will be soon. No one will ever find you. The only thing you have to worry about is how much pain you have to suffer before you die. Now I have a few questions. If you answer honestly you'll die quickly. If you lie to me I'll cause you a great deal of pain. The sort of pain I hear your friends like to inflict on defenceless Welshmen."

Jorge looked into the eyes of the man standing over him and knew he was not joking. This man meant business. Jorge knew he was a dead man.

Owain came over and started a small fire a few feet from the prone rider. Some of the other men carried the dead bodies into the woods. Jorge could see them stripping the dead of their arms and valuables. He groaned as the arrows in him ached.

Ednyfed reached forward and pulled an arrow from Jorge's flesh and Jorge screamed as the pain coursed through him. Ednyfed squatted by the wounded man and tossed the arrow to Owain.

"Hurts, doesn't it?" he asked rhetorically. "Why did you shoot my son?"

"I didn't," Jorge replied.

Ednyfed smiled, "Well, when he left home he didn't have a hole in his shoulder, now he has a very nasty hole where he was hit by an arrow from behind. So don't tell me you didn't shoot him. Are you Gaspard?"

Jorge was surprised at the mention of Gaspard's name. "No."

"Who are you then?" demanded Ednyfed.

"Jorge of Aquitaine, in the service of Lord de Grey," replied the sergeant, knowing that nothing he said would prevent his death and the only way his pain would be relieved was to tell this man what he wanted to know.

"So, Jorge, why is your Lord de Grey hunting my son?"

"We're not. We're hunting a messenger."

"Well, you shot my son and I'm not very happy about that. Who is Gaspard?"

"He's a sergeant-at-arms. He and two archers shot your son because they thought he was the messenger Lord de Grey wanted."

"Why didn't they just ask him instead of just trying to kill him?"

"You'd have to ask Gaspard that," said Jorge defiantly. Ednyfed reached forward and applied some pressure to one of Jorge's wounds and the man screamed.

"I suppose I will," said Ednyfed. "Where are Lord de Grey and this Gaspard now?"

"They were at Ludlow Castle yesterday; I can't say where they are now."

The Welshman made no comment but just watched Jorge like a cat watching a trapped mouse.

"Lord de Grey wants the messenger before he moves north to his castle at Ruthin," said Jorge, hoping that the Welshman would finish him off quickly.

Ednyfed nodded to Owain and Owain drew a sharp dagger from his boot sheath. He took hold of Jorge by the shoulder and rolled him face down into the mud. He pulled back Jorge's head by his hair and drew the blade across Jorge's throat, severing his windpipe and jugular vein. The blood spurted out onto the ground and Jorge died with a hollow sigh.

Owain stripped Jorge of his weapons and armour as the war party gathered round the fire.

Two horses had to be put down because of their wounds but the others were good to travel. The arms and equipment was sorted and piled by the fire ready for loading. One of the horsemen was sent to bring their horses from the other side of the hill. The men sat down to clean their weapons while Ednyfed and Owain discussed what they were going to do next.

Ednyfed decided that two men should take the horses and the arms back to the camp at Offa's Dyke as they would only slow the raiding party down. He would lead the rest of the men to the place where Caradoc's pack was hidden.

Huw led the party that buried Lord de Grey's men in a pit in the forest. Gwillym and Rhodri rounded up the horses taken from Lord de Grey's men and loaded them with the spare arms and armour.

"Take those horses back to the border; we don't want any animals that can be recognised with us if we have ride into Ludlow," said Ednyfed. "If we are not back at Offa's Dyke by tomorrow take the horses and arms to the hill fort south of Llanmerwig and wait for us there."

It was getting dark as the two men headed back to the border. Travelling at night round Clun would allow them to avoid awkward questions from the Clun garrison.

Ednyfed called the men to him. "Check the ground and make sure all evidence of what happen here is gone. Burn any clothing and broken arrow shafts. Collect any arrow heads that can be reused. The rain will wash away the blood but clear away anything else."

"Huw, ride to Clun and go to the inn of the Raven and tell Glyn that Lord Grey's men will trouble him no more. Tell him to be careful with that castellan." Huw mounted his horse and Ednyfed continued, "Make sure you are not seen and be back here before day break."

Huw nodded and galloped away, riding back to the main road between Clun and Ludlow. He wanted to make the best use of what daylight was left.

They set up camp in the valley overnight so that they would not get caught moving on the road. Ednyfed set two men to keep watch while the others slept. The guards changed every two hours so that everyone got some sleep. The valley was quiet and secluded so they were not disturbed by any traffic on the road between Clun and Ludlow.

They missed the messenger Lord de Grey sent to tell Jorge to return to Ludlow. The messenger was dismayed at what appeared to be Jorge's desertion with his whole troop. He returned to Ludlow and gave Lord de Grey the news that Jorge and his men had disappeared into the Clun Forest still hunting the messenger.

Nobody noticed the lone horseman in the trees, he just watched and waited. He observed the raiding party mount up and ride out of the valley with one man left to brush away their tracks.

He rode up the valley and searched the area. He found the fire where the clothes of Lord de Grey's men had been burned and the pit where the bodies were buried. The work had been hurried; however, who would come searching this remote valley for a patrol of English men-at-arms?

He salvaged part of a tabard with Lord de Grey's insignia on it. He tucked it away into the bottom of his saddle bag. The man rode round the valley, checking the tracks that had been left. He was soon sure that the ambush would not be discovered and rode to the Ludlow road, following the tracks of the raiding party as they headed east.

Black Hill – Stanton Lacy

Before sunrise Ednyfed had his men in the saddle heading east for the escarpment where Caradoc had been attacked and wounded. They had no time for breakfast, just a cup of water and some oat cakes as they rode. They crossed the Teme as the sun was rising in the east but the valleys were shrouded in fog, giving the land an eerie feel. The weather had taken a colder turn and the bottom of the valley near the river was still covered by thick fog. The raiding party circled to the north and followed a sheep track up onto the escarpment.

Owain followed Caradoc's directions to the place where he had left his pack in the undergrowth. Owain soon found the pack hidden in some bushes several yards back from the ridge where he could see the outcropping Caradoc had been standing on when he was shot. He pulled the pack out and opened it. It had his brother's best tunic at the top so he repacked it and lashed it to his saddle. He checked the ground where the pack had been hidden to make sure nothing else was still left in the hiding place. His brother's bow was still missing; it must have gone over the edge with him.

Owain walked to where Ednyfed was sitting on his horse. "Should we go down the escarpment to find his bow and arrow bag?"

"I think not. If Grey's men were searching for him they almost certainly found them, and I don't want to waste too much time up here – we don't know how many men Grey has with him and I'm not going to get caught in the open by a troop of knights." Ednyfed turned his head as if he had heard something. He waved his hand and the men disbursed into the trees to hide and wait.

Two archers on horseback came into view, riding along the edge of the escarpment. They had their hoods up against the wind blowing in from the south-west. They were clearly looking for something along the edge of the escarpment and eventually they stopped at a point on the ridge near the outcropping Caradoc had told them about. The taller man passed his reins to his companion and dismounted.

He walked to a tree and started to pull a rope up. He cursed as it got snagged on the undergrowth. "Give me a hand will you, William?"

"Pass the rope up and I'll get the horse to pull it clear," said the older man.

"Trust Gaspard to remember the rope, he's a mean bastard," said Jared, the younger archer, as he pulled the rope up and passed the end to William.

William took the rope and tied the end to his saddle. He walked his horse slowly away from the edge of the escarpment. The rope came up and Jared pulled on it. As soon as he had the end of the rope he stared to coil it. William rode back, untied the rope from his saddle and dismounted.

"You should be pleased to be here and not with the rest of the men riding with his lordship in the mood he's in. We can catch up with them by nightfall but our journey will be easier for not having to ride in formation. And we can stop at an ale house on the way," William said with the smile of an old soldier who knows how to have a good skive. "That'll warm you up."

Owain listened to their conversation from where he was lying in the undergrowth. He moved closer to the sound of the men talking. Jared had nearly coiled the rope when Owain rose up and hit him had on his head with his falchion. It bounced off the man's helmet, cutting deeply into his shoulder, breaking his collarbone as if it was a twig.

Jared screamed in pain and William tried to draw his sword but two of Ednyfed's men landed on him, knocking him to the ground. William struggled but was soon tied with the rope. Jared had blood pouring from his wound and was in no state to fight. Owain caught him another blow to the head, knocking off his helmet. He forced Jared to the ground and used a bowstring to secure his hands.

Owain stood up and kicked Jared in his ribs; there was a sound of bones breaking. Owain was about to kick him again when Ednyfed dismounted and pushed his son away. "Let's hear what they have to say before you kill them, shall we?"

Owain stepped back, putting his falchion away after cleaning the blood from it. Ednyfed knelt down by Jared and inspected the wound. "You'll bleed to death if you don't get to a surgeon."

Jared said nothing but William said, "Do you know who we serve? Lord Reginald de Grey will have your heads for this."

Ednyfed turned his head to look at the older archer. He stood up and walked to William's horse. There he found his bow and his arrow bag. He took an arrow from the bag and looked at the arrow head. He took an arrow head from his pouch and held them together.

"They look very similar to me. Do you know where I got this?" he asked William, indicating to the arrow head. William shook his head but he could guess.

"My son had this in his pouch. He said he kept it after he got the arrow out of his shoulder. Would you like to tell me why he had it in his shoulder?"

William immediately knew he was a dead man. Jared had passed out with his pain and so Ednyfed turned his attention to William. "Tell me what happened on this ridge when you tried to kill my son."

William kept silent. He was frantically thinking what story he should tell.

"Who is Gaspard?" Ednyfed demanded.

The name surprised William, *how did they know the sergeant's name?*

"He's one of Lord de Grey's sergeants-at-arms. He commands his lordship's bowmen," answered William trying to think of a way to buy some time. "They're going north to his lordship's estates at Ruthin."

"Why were you and the boy sent to get the rope?"

"I'll not say more until you get some help for the boy."

Ednyfed nodded to Owain who drew out his boot knife. "He'll cut your friend to pieces bit by bit for what you did to his brother, and then he'll start on you. He's very fond of his older brother." Ednyfed left his comment hanging in the air.

"Gaspard said Lord de Grey was expecting a messenger going across the border into Wales. He wanted the message he's carrying. When Gaspard saw the man on the skyline he thought he had to be the messenger. He was travelling light, he didn't even have a pack, so we thought that he must be the man we wanted."

"You just didn't see his pack, it's there." Owain pointed to the pack tied behind his saddle. "Why didn't you just ask him who he was and where he was going before shooting him?"

William squirmed but the rope held him tightly. "Gaspard said shoot him, so we did. You don't argue with the sergeant."

"So you just shoot anyone who happens to be passing, it doesn't matter if you have the right man or not," Owain stated angrily, taking a step towards the old archer.

The men had gathered round the two Englishmen. Ednyfed looked about. "Who's keeping watch?" He pointed at two men. "You two go and keep a look out to the south." He selected two more men to guard the north and waved them in that direction. The men walked away, unlimbering their bows. "Form a skirmish line and keep your horses with you. I don't think we'll be here much longer."

He returned his attention to William and Jared. He inspected Jared's wound and as he did so undid the wounded man's belt, tossing it to one side. He probed the wound and then looked at William. "He has a broken collarbone and that cut is very deep. With the amount of blood he's lost I think he's dead."

William groaned and cursed Gaspard under his breath.

"I can make his passing swift or I can just leave him here to bleed to death, but I can't travel with a man this badly wounded."

"I could take him to Ludlow," said William, hoping to escape his captors.

"I think not. I want more answers from you and when I've finished with you I may ransom you back to Lord Grey if he'll pay. What are you worth to him?"

"Make his passing quick then," said William mournfully.

Owain dragged Jared to the edge of the escarpment and stabbed him from behind. He felt the young man's neck; there was no pulse. His chest no longer rose and fell dragging in each ragged breath. Owain stripped Jared of his gear and rolled the body over the edge. The corpse rolled down into the undergrowth and came to rest beneath the trees.

"Aren't you going to bury him?" William accused.

"We don't have time," said Ednyfed bluntly.

"But the foxes will get him."

"Not our problem," said Owain as he hauled William to his feet and stuffed a rag into his mouth, and tied another rag around his mouth to keep the other one in place. "Breathe through your nose or you'll suffocate," advised Owain.

He dragged William to his horse and threw him over the saddle. Owain tied him across the saddle while William made protesting noises.

One of Ednyfed's men suggested, "You could let him ride."

"He'll be less trouble this way," said Owain as he tied William's and feet together under the horse's belly.

Ednyfed whistled and the outlying sentries came running back to join the rest of the men as they mounted to move back towards the border. Ednyfed had one more place he wanted to visit before they started their sweep back down the western side of Offa's Dyke.

They left the escarpment by the northern track and headed west in the direction Caradoc had taken after he had been shot.

Will's farm, Shropshire

Will had risen early because he was worried when Kate had not returned from Ludlow the night before. She should have been back the previous day and she did not know many people in Ludlow so he did not know where she could have spent the night.

He fed his animals and made sure everything was in order and then he set off for the town and he was waiting at the Broad Gate when the gatekeeper opened it just after sunrise.

"You're early this morning, Will. We don't often see you in town."

"I thought I'd beat the crowds," said Will as he passed through the gate. He knew the gatekeeper because the man's father had a farm near his own. He thought about asking the man if he'd seen Kate the previous day but decided against it because the man would spread the rumour round the town that Will couldn't keep his wife at home. So he formulated another question.

"Do you still have Lord de Grey and his men imposing themselves on you at the castle? They seem like a rowdy lot."

"They left this morning for the north and I will not be the only one happy to see the back of his lordship and his henchman, Gaspard. That bastard's always creeping about; even his own men don't like him. The castle can get back to normal now he's gone. He had men riding out at all times of day and night. The disruption they have caused ruined the Castle routine and they've caused so much bad feeling with the peasants."

"What were they looking for?" asked Will innocently.

"Who, not what, but a whole patrol of about ten men has gone missing. They rode to Clun but they've not returned."

"They could have joined his lordship on his way to Shrewsbury or gone on ahead of him," suggested Will.

"You're probably right," shrugged the gatekeeper as he secured the gate to the wall.

Will nodded and walked up the hill towards the town square. He suddenly had a terrible thought, *What if Kate came to try and collect the reward for the wounded boy?* He quickened his pace up the hill. In the town square some of the traders were opening up their stalls. Will asked a mercer if he had seen his wife on the previous day.

"What does she look like?"

"A bit shorter than me with blonde hair. She was wearing a dark brown cloak and was carrying a basket of eggs."

"I could be wrong but I did see a woman of that description hanging round the castle gatehouse. She looked as if she couldn't make her mind up about something. I didn't see her when I was locking up so she was gone by dusk."

"Thank you, you've been most helpful," said Will, the mercer having confirmed Will's worst nightmare. How was he going to find out if she was still being held in the castle? *You stupid woman,* he thought.

He could not do any more in the town so he hurried back to his farm. What was wrong with her? Why couldn't she leave it alone? Now he would probably lose his farm as well as his wife. He would be lucky if he got away with his life. It was never good policy to seek the attention of a marcher lord and definitely not this particular marcher lord: Lord de Grey was known for his ruthlessness.

Will had not been back at his farm long when he heard some horses arrive in the yard. He came out of the house expecting to see Lord de Grey's men but instead there was a troop of horsemen he did not recognise. Two men dismounted and the leader waved the rest of the men into the barn out of sight of the road.

Ednyfed introduced himself. "I'm Ednyfed, the father of the boy you helped on his way to the border."

Will sighed with relief; he did not want to have to deal with Lord de Grey's men if he could avoid it. He crossed the yard and counted the number of men as he held out his hand to the leader. Will grasped Ednyfed's hand and said, "I have some ale in the house."

Ednyfed and his men followed Will into the house and out of sight of the road. He poured small ale for each man and most of the men went back out to mind their horses in the barn.

Owain and Huw stayed with Ednyfed in the farm's warm kitchen. The men sipped their beer and Will waited to find out what the Welshmen wanted.

When Ednyfed had slaked his thirst he put his tankard down on the table and asked, "Do you know why Lord Grey had my son shot?"

"I don't know. Jorge, his sergeant, did not say why either. He and his men were just searching for your son although I think I heard one of his men refer to your son as the messenger."

"That's what we heard in Clun, but the boy has no knowledge of any message, he was just travelling on his way home from Oxford where he was visiting his uncle. Can you spread the word that the boy wasn't a messenger?" asked Ednyfed.

"I don't get to town much. The person to spread that information is my wife; she wouldn't thank me for saying it but she's a bit of a gossip." Will paused and took a deep breath. "The only trouble is Kate went to Ludlow the day before yesterday and she hasn't returned. I went to the town this morning to find her. A trader I know saw her by the main castle gate. I think she's been taken but I don't know what to do about it. If I complain to the Earl of Arundel he'll probably blame me for not keeping her at home and I don't want to lose my farm." Will was surprised at what he had just told these strangers.

Ednyfed looked meaningfully at Owain.

The younger man asked, "Who was the trader you spoke to? Tell me exactly what he said."

Will reiterated what the mercer had told him and Owain nodded as he listened. He thought for a few moments and looked at Huw. "What we need is a reason to get into the gatehouse."

"How about a body with an arrow through its shoulder," said Huw. Owain nodded but did not explain more, reading Huw's thoughts. "We will go to the castle and send word when we find your wife. If she was taken by Grey's men it may not be pretty," he warned.

"I just want her back with no fuss," said Will, just wanting the return of his wife.

"I can't guarantee no fuss but I will make every effort to find her. We owe you that for helping Caradoc. Can you describe your wife to me?"

"She's a bit shorter than me with blond hair and very blue eyes. She's slim but stronger than she looks. She's only two-and-twenty and as I say, she talks too much. "

"What was she wearing when she left?" asked Owain.

"A long brown cloak and a blue dress, and she wore boots because of the walk."

"Does she have any distinguishing features like a scar or a birthmark that would give us a positive identification?"

Will could see the young man was serious about finding his wife but had to think hard to think of something that would distinguish her from any other blonde woman in the town, especially for a man who had never met her.

"Is there something we could ask her that only she would know? Her day of birth, the day you wed, something like that?" Owain pressed for detail.

"She was born two days after Valentine's day in the town of Kidderminster. We were married two years ago and she has a birthmark on her shoulder." He turned and pointed at his shoulder blade. "It's shaped like a harp." He drew the shape with his finger on the table top.

Owain waited to see if Will had any more to say. When nothing was forthcoming he looked at Huw and said, "We'd best be off."

Ednyfed nodded and said he would see them outside.

When Owain and Huw had gone he turned to Will and said, "I know this must be hard but as soon as we know anything we'll send word."

"Thank you." Will did not know what else to say.

"When we find her you may need to come quickly and you may have to come to Wales to get her. I want to know what Lord Grey wanted with my youngest boy. So we'll be travelling fast. We may have to just cut and run but you have my word I will let you know if we find her." Ednyfed paused and then said bluntly, "I think you should prepare for the worst and hope for the best. Have your horse ready and have someone here to look after your farm. If you need to get a message to me in future go to Glyn at The Raven in Clun. He can get a message to me across the border."

Ednyfed tried to smile but his smile looked like a grimace. "We are both the victims here and I owe you for helping the boy. So if you need me let me know and I will come."

Ednyfed opened the door and waved to Owain who rode over to him. Will came to the doorway and watched the riders as they prepared to leave. Owain nodded at his father's instructions and rode off with Huw and another rider.

Ednyfed took the rest of his men and started north towards Shrewsbury.

Ludlow

Huw and Owain made good time in returning to the base of the escarpment where Jared's body had been thrown. Iolo found the body and Huw dragged it out of the trees. They looked at the man's broken body, now drained of blood.

"It'll have to do," said Owain, drawing an arrow.

Iolo and Huw held the body up while Owain fired an arrow into the body's shoulder from behind. They broke off the arrow, leaving part of the shaft in the wound, and then heaved the body onto Owain's horse and tied him there.

Iolo and Owain doubled up to ride to Ludlow. Before they got to the town gate Owain dismounted and led his horse forward on foot. Iolo and Huw rode south around the town and entered by Broad Gate. They were in the castle square in front of the main gate five minutes before Owain trudged past The Bull Ring tavern and into Castle Square. Owain went straight to the castle's main gate, while Huw and Iolo watched from either side of the square. Both men had their bows strung with arrows ready but not nocked, just in case Owain needed some help.

At the gate Owain banged his fist on the door and a guard appeared. The guard looked at Owain and then at the half naked body draped over the horse.

"I hear you're looking for a man with an arrow in his shoulder," said Owain.

"That was Lord de Grey," answered the guard.

"I was told the lord of the castle at Ludlow wanted this man. It was said in Clun." Owain's look challenged the guard to disagree with him. A sergeant came out of the gate on hearing the sound of raised voices.

Owain turned to the sergeant and said, "I've come for the reward for this man." He slipped the knot on the rope holding the body in place across the saddle and the body slipped to the ground in the middle of the gateway.

"You can't leave that there," said the sergeant, pointing at the body.

At that moment they heard horses arriving in the square as Sir Edmund Mortimer and some of his men arrived.

"What's going on here?" he demanded as he pulled his horse to a halt beside Owain's.

The sergeant stepped forward and said, "This man is claiming a reward for bringing us this body. It's the messenger Lord de Grey was searching for."

"Why did Lord Reginald want this man?" demanded Sir Edmund.

"He thought he was a messenger, my lord."

"Well he's nothing now, is he? Get him out of here – I don't want bodies lying about in the town square." He turned in his saddle and looked at Owain. "Take the body to the graveyard. Robert, go with him and then bring him to see me when you've given the body to the sexton."

Sir Edmund rode through the gate followed by his retinue. The sergeant helped Robert and Owain get the body back onto the horse and Robert led Owain back across the square and out of town towards the graveyard.

Owain struck up a conversation with Robert as they walked. "You didn't sound as if you enjoyed Lord Grey's visit."

"He's an arrogant bastard, that's for sure, but some of his men are worse."

"What do you mean?" probed Owain.

"One of his sergeants-at-arms was a real mean bastard. He tortured a woman for most of the night trying to get her to tell where this messenger was hiding." He waved his hand towards the corpse. "Where did you find him?"

"He tried to take my horse the other side of Clun. I hit him with my falchion; you can see where I hit him on the shoulder."

"And then you stabbed him," added Robert, looking down at the corpse.

"I hoped you hadn't noticed that but a dead man's easier to handle than a live one, especially if he's on the run," said Owain pragmatically.

They found the sexton in the graveyard digging a grave. He climbed out of the hole to look at the body as Owain pulled it off the horse.

"No relatives?" asked the sexton.

"Not that we know of. He's the messenger Lord de Grey was looking for," said Robert.

The sexton searched the body but found nothing of value. He looked about and dragged the body away and laid it out by the wall. He got a sack cloth and covered it.

"Who is paying for the burial?"

"The parish," answered Robert, knowing that the earl would not want to pay. "You could try Lord de Grey; he was keen to get his hands on him."

The sexton snorted and jumped back into his hole to finish his digging.

Robert looked at Owain and nodded his head in the direction of the castle. They left the sexton digging as they made their way back up the hill to the square.

When they reached The Feathers, Owain said, "I'll just stable my horse."

"No, you will not," said the guard, taking hold of the reins.

"He needs some grain and a rub down," said Owain, patting the horse's neck.

"We have stables in the castle and you are to be Sir Edmund's guest for the night," said Robert emphatically.

Owain let the reins drop and followed Robert past The Bull Ring back to the castle. Robert led the way into the outer bailey and showed Owain where he could stable his horse.

While Owain was rubbing down his horse he encouraged Robert to talk about Gaspard and what he had done to the woman.

"She not here any more, Gaspard put her in the back of one of their wagons. I think he gave her something because she didn't make a sound when they left."

Owain tossed some hay for his horse and filled a nose bag with oats. When he was finished Owain followed Robert to the small bridge which crossed a ditch to the entrance tower that led into the inner bailey.

They passed the small round Norman church and Robert showed Owain into the main hall. Sir Edmund and his men were at table eating when Robert led Owain into the hall. They stood in front of the high table until Sir Edmund noticed them. He finished his leg of chicken and tossed the bones to one of the hounds that were prowling round the tables, begging for scraps.

"You got rid of the body?" said Sir Edmund.

Robert answered, "The sexton wanted to know who was paying for the burial. So I told him to charge Lord Grey."

Sir Edmund, who had just taken a gulp of wine, started to laugh and he spewed the wine out over the floor so that Robert and Owain had to jump out of the way to avoid the spray. He was choking, so Owain reached out and pulled him over the table and slapped him on his back. The earl coughed up some chicken and spat it onto the floor. He continued coughing but soon got himself under control.

"Take some deep breaths," said Owain as he supported Sir Edmund.

He wiped his face with a cloth and poured himself some more wine. He took a sip and walked away towards the fireplace. Robert and Owain followed.

"Robert, get yourself and this man a drink. I want to know how came you by the body of Lord de Grey's messenger." He sat down on a bench and indicated that Owain should do the same. "Well?" said Sir Edmund.

Robert passed Owain a tankard of ale and he took a sip. It was beer so he took a good swig and made up his story.

"I was riding home from Montgomery when I was accosted by the man. I think he was out of his mind. He attacked me with a staff – I think he was after my horse. So I struck out with my falchion and caught him on the shoulder. I broke his collarbone and he bled like a stuck pig so I did the merciful thing and finished him off."

"Why did you bring him here?" asked Sir Edmund.

"I was in Clun two days ago and some of Lord de Grey's men were searching people on the road, looking for a man with an arrow in his shoulder. Seeing the wound in my attacker's shoulder I could only assume he was the one they were looking for. So I brought him here because Lord de Grey's man, Jorge, said there would be a reward."

Sir Edmund smiled. "Reginald, give a reward? You don't know him very well, do you? Hell will freeze first."

Sir Edmund looked at Robert. "Do you believe him?"

"No reason not to, my lord," said the guard who had come to like the young man while they had been together disposing of the body.

"Who are you?"

"I'm Owain ap Ednyfed from the Vale of Ceri," said Owain.

"And what are you doing this side of the border?"

"I was collecting some debts for my father, but I haven't been very successful yet, that's why the reward would have come in handy," lied Owain.

"Have some food and Robert will show you where you can sleep. I'll not reward you for killing that man but I'll not condemn you for it either because he was a fugitive and from the sound of it you were just defending yourself." Sir Edmund turned to Robert, "I think you should relieve him of his falchion but he can have it back when he leaves in the morning."

Owain passed his falchion to the guard and the knight stood up. He looked at Owain, sizing him up. "Come and see me in the morning before you go. I think we may be of use to each other and I may be able to help you with the funds you have yet to collect."

Robert found a bunk for Owain in the barracks and left him to sleep.

Robert shook Owain awake at sunrise. Owain rolled over and sat up and pulled on his boots. He followed Robert to the table where there was fresh bread and meats from the previous night's meal. Owain helped himself to some food, washing it down with a drink from a pitcher of milk.

When they had eaten Robert tugged at Owain's sleeve to indicate that he should follow him from the barracks. Once they were outside in the bailey he said under his breath, "His lordship wants a quiet word and then you can leave."

Owain nodded and followed Robert into the inner bailey to the small round Norman church. There they found Sir Edmund with Thomas, Earl of Arundel, who was on his knees, praying. They waited for him to finish. The earl got up from his knees and dismissed Robert with a wave of his hand. "Stand guard outside and see we are not disturbed."

The earl turned to Owain and indicated that he should take a seat beside him. "I find this a good place to have private discussions away from prying eyes."

Owain did not respond.

The earl continued, "I've heard some rumours about a band of armed Welshmen running around southern Shropshire. Know anything about it?"

Again Owain did not respond; he kept his face straight showing nothing. The earl watched Owain's face carefully.

"Mmmmm," the earl mused. "Lord de Grey wouldn't have anything to do with it, would he?

The earl waited for Owain to respond but the Welshman said nothing.

"I'll make some statements and you can agree or not but I will draw my own conclusions," said the earl as he glanced sideways and Sir Edmund.

There was no change in Owain's expression.

"The castellan at Clun informs me that a sergeant-at-arms in the service of Lord de Grey and some of his men have gone missing." The earl paused and there was still no response from the Welshman. "You wouldn't know anything about that, would you?"

"I have never met Lord de Grey," said Owain.

The earl continued, "That's not what I asked. I hear there was a search for a wounded man."

"Oh! I heard that in an inn from a man called Jorge," Owain mumbled.

"Do you know who he was?"

The earl watched the young man's eyes to see if he would give anything away. Nothing.

"One of my tenants has had several visits from troops of armed horsemen. I think one of those troops was our friend Jorge. Do you know who the others were?" asked Sir Edmund.

Not a word came from Owain, though he would tell his father that for further incursions into England they would have to be more careful. He concentrated on keeping his face straight and not showing any emotion.

"And now you turn up with a dead man who could be the fugitive. And after Lord de Grey and so many of his men couldn't find him. I don't suppose you know why he was so important to Lord de Grey?"

"No, my lord," responded Owain.

As the earl could see no answer was forthcoming, he continued, "I could have you tortured."

"And you would learn nothing, because I know only what I told Sir Edmund last night," said Owain.

"Oh, I'm sure I would learn something but probably not what I would want to hear. I like you my boy and so I'm going to give you some advice. Finish whatever business you have here and go back to Wales and stay there." He leaned forward and put his hands on Owain's shoulders and stared into his eyes. "And don't raid any of my lands or I'll come after you. Understand."

Owain's control almost snapped but he bit his lip and some blood appeared on his lips. The earl studied the younger man's face. He took in every line and crease. He stared into Owain's green eyes and saw the strength there, and knew he would get nothing from this man.

"When you are ready I want you to come and talk with me at Shrewsbury. I rule this part of the border and I think we have much in common. Do you know Lord Rhys who lives the other side of Caersws?"

The question caught Owain off guard and he said, "I know of him. I've seen him at the market in Newtown. I don't know him to talk to."

"Good. I suggest you go and talk to him and when you do ask him about me." The earl released his grip on Owain's shoulders and stood up. "I think we have an understanding. Take care on your journey and I look forward to our next meeting."

Owain stood up. "Thank you for the bed and board. I too look forward to our next meeting. Can I leave now?"

The earl took a small purse from his pouch and tossed it to Owain. He caught it deftly wit his left hand. Owain looked in askance at the earl.

"Let's call it some expenses."

Owain was at a loss for something to say.

"Let's say it's the reward for finding Lord de Grey's fugitive," said the earl, "but somehow I don't think the man buried in the churchyard is the one Lord de Grey was trying to find."

Owain understood the warning the earl was giving him. The earl was telling him he that knew exactly what was going on in his territory.

"I understand, my lord," said Owain as he bowed and walked out of the small round church.

Robert took him back out to the outer bailey where Owain's horse was already saddled and waiting. He mounted his horse and Robert passed his falchion back to him and he slid it back into his belt.

"Farewell. I hope you have a good journey home," said the guard.

"I still have an errand to run before I see my home but I thank you for your hospitality." Owain walked his horse to the gate and the guard let him out. He rode out across the square, noting that Huw was still at his post, watching. Owain showed him no sign of recognition as he rode across the square and down the street to Broad Gate.

Huw waited for ten minutes and saw a small troop of four men follow Owain. Huw went to The Bull Ring and rousted Iolo out of his bed and they rode north out of the town to catch up with Owain on the journey north to meet with Ednyfed.

Cudlow Castle

In the round chapel of St Mary Magdalene two men sat in silence. The silence was enhanced by the four foot thick walls. It was a good place to have a confidential conversation without the walls having ears.

The Earl of Arundel was contemplating the meeting they had just had with the young Welshman. He glanced at the west door as Robert returned to report that Owain had left the castle.

"What did you think of him?" the earl asked the guard.

"Dangerous, ruthless and I think he knows more than he was saying," replied Robert. "But he took very good care of his horse." As if this would redeem the Welshman's character.

"You spent time with him last night, what did he have say for himself?" asked Sir Edmund, having placed Robert with Owain to try and draw the Welshman out.

"He spoke little but asked questions about Gaspard, Lord de Grey's sergeant. That's why I think he knows more than he was saying."

Sir Edmund smiled. "So he got more information from you than you did from him?"

Robert blushed and stammered, "I don't think so, my lord. He only asked about Lord de Grey and about why he wanted the man he brought in. I thought I could get him to drink more but he just went to sleep."

"So we're none the wiser," said the earl. "What does Reginald think he's playing at? He can't go round just killing yeomen as he likes." He looked up at Robert. "Our men followed Owain ap whatever?"

"Yes, my lord, they followed him as he left the town."

"Good, maybe they will find something worth knowing. You can go," said the earl, dismissing Robert. The guard turn and left the chapel by the west door and closed it firmly behind him.

Sir Edmund stood up and paced along the nave. The earl stayed seated.

"What do you think?" asked the earl.

"I think de Grey has gone mad but I wouldn't say that before the king," the knight responded. "Remember the king is holding my nephew."

"Yes, I know, it can't be easy for you knowing the boy is hostage with the king. However, Reginald's getting more and more out of control. What do you think he will do next?" asked the earl, testing his friend.

"I don't know but I just hope it's far away from here, hopefully in Scotland with the king on hand to see him."

"That's a nice idea but I think that whatever Reginald did in Scotland it would be fine by Henry. He wants to punish the Scots for their impudence." The earl was silent while he thought. "I just hope you're right, but I have a feeling in my water that he's doing something in Wales we are all going to regret."

"What do you think that would be?"

"I just don't know but I don't want him disrupting our Welsh troops. They were the best part of the army the last time we ventured north. I wouldn't want them deserting because Reginald has done something stupid here."

"Can you not influence the king to keep de Grey under control?" asked Sir Edmund, who was worried about his own men, many of whom were Welsh.

"I've tried but he will not listen to me as King Richard listened to my father. And remember how he ruled Brecon when he was still the Duke of Lancaster? They still remember him there with bad feelings. The Welsh have long memories; they pass on feuds from father to son like we pass lands and titles," explained the earl.

"I suppose all we can do is wait and see what he does."

"We can distance ourselves from him, not that I'm sure that will do us much good. If the king goes to war in Wales we will be in the front line and there's nothing we can do about it. What's more, Henry of Monmouth is Prince of Wales now and is responsible, with young Percy's guidance, with keeping Wales under control."

"We'd better prepare for war then."

"That would be prudent, I think."

The earl rose and Sir Edmund joined him, leaving the chapel by the west door leading into the inner bailey.

They left the small chapel to its silence.

Frankwell, Shrewsbury

Huw and Iolo were waiting on the road near Stokesay Manor, the home of the merchant Lawrence of Ludlow, for Owain to arrive after he circled round Ludlow, leaving a westward trail towards the border. Huw wanted to know what had happened in the castle but Owain wanted to move on to meet his father as quickly as possible.

They rode north to Shrewsbury which Llywelyn ab Iorwerth had tried to capture, and where his brother Dafydd was hung, drawn and quartered by the English on the High Cross on Pride Hill, not far from the red sandstone castle which was built by the Normans. So the town was one well know to the Welshmen for the barbarity of the English as well as the trade in woollens and other goods.

As they rode along the western side of the river they could see the town in the ox-bow of the river Severn. There were all manner of buildings in the town, from small wooded shacks to imposing town and guild houses.

The three Welshmen passed the stone bridge which was fortified with its tower and gatehouse. The entered the area on the north-western side of the town known as Frankwell in search of The Buck inn. The Frankwell area was an area where traders did not pay the town levy on sales and it was situated on the Welsh side of the river Severn, a free town. They found the tavern and Iolo took the horses to the stables while Huw and Owain went to find Ednyfed.

They ordered some food and Huw badgered Owain to tell him what had happened in Ludlow Castle.

"I'll tell you and my father at the same time to save repeating myself," said the younger man, wondering whether he should include his interview in the Norman church with the Earl of Arundel and Sir Edmund Mortimer.

Ednyfed returned to the inn as they finished eating their food. He had left men watching the tavern in the town where Lord de Grey's men were billeted. Lord de Grey himself was at the castle but Gaspard was staying at the inn in the town.

"What did you find out in Ludlow?" asked Ednyfed.

"Lord Grey's sergeant Gaspard certainly questioned a woman who answers the description of Will's wife and according to Robert the guard he seemed to take pleasure in tormenting and torturing her. Robert told me Gaspard put the woman in the back of a wagon when Lord Grey and his men left Ludlow to go north to Shrewsbury."

"I thought they'd arrested you when you dropped the corpse of the dead archer," said Huw as he couldn't contain himself.

"That was a disagreement about the reward for the man Lord Grey was chasing. The earl was not interested in Lord Grey's fugitive, but I think Sir Edmund might have been. That's why we took the archer to the churchyard for a pauper's burial. It gave me a chance to talk to Robert, one of the guards. He obviously didn't like Lord Grey or his men, and Gaspard seemed to be the worst. The man's a bully and Lord Grey doesn't restrain him. I met Arundel this morning and he gave me a warning and this."

He dropped the coin purse on the table.

Owain took a sip of his ale and continued, "I don't think there's much love lost between the Earl of Arundel's men and Lord Grey's. Lord Arundel is playing a different game altogether. I also think Sir Edmund is in Arundel's camp."

He let his comment sink in and then continued. "Robert told me about Jorge going missing and I suggested that he had gone north to meet Lord Grey, but I'm not sure if he believed me."

"Did you speak to Sir Edmund?" asked Ednyfed.

"Yes, he arrived at the castle just after I arrived with the corpse of our friend. When we had taken the body to the sexton, Robert took me to the Great Hall where Sir Edmund was dining. He asked me some questions and then warned me about raiding his lands."

"Why didn't you come out of the castle last night?" asked Huw.

"Because I was with Robert and I was taken to sleep in the barracks in the outer bailey. I think Sir Edmund was doing some checking and this morning Robert came down and let me go." Owain decided not to recant his conversation with the other earl in the little Norman church. He turned to his father and asked, "What have you found out about Lord Grey, Gaspard and Will's wife?"

"Lord Grey is at the castle but his men are billeted at several inns in the town. Gaspard is at The Lion on Wyle Cop. I have two men watching the inn so we'll know if he makes a move."

"We need to know if he still has the woman and if he has where he's keeping her. We need someone to go into the inn and find his room and the stables in case he's got her hidden there. From what Robert was saying I don't think she's in any state to be seen in public, that's why they took her with them from Ludlow hidden in the back of a cart."

Iolo entered the inn having curried the horses. He sat down next to Ednyfed and waved to a serving wench to bring him food and a tankard of ale.

"You'd better get that down you quickly, I have a job for you," said Ednyfed.

"That sounds ominous," said Iolo as he started eating.

"We need to find Will's wife. We know where Gaspard is, so we need either to grab him and make him tell us or we need to find the woman and take her to Shrewsbury Abbey, where she'll be safe until Will can collect her. Once we've got her we need to send a message to Will to come for her."

Iolo finished his food and the four men walked across the stone bridge and into the town. They made their way through the narrow streets to Wyle Cop where Iolo went to the rear of the inn and searched the stables. Huw waited in the street while Ednyfed and Owain went into the inn.

There were groups of men sitting drinking, several of them in Lord Grey's livery. Owain, who spoke the better English, ordered two tankards of ale. Ednyfed led the way to a seat near a window. He spotted Gaspard sitting with a group of men on the far side of the inn. He recognised him because the other men deferred to him.

One of Ednyfed's men was sitting on his own by the door that led upstairs to the bedrooms.

Iolo came in through the rear door and shook his head. He ordered a drink from a passing serving girl and joined his friend by the rear door. After fifteen minutes Owain asked where the privy was and went out of the door at the rear of the inn.

Instead of going out of the rear of the inn to where the privy was located he bounded up the stairs to the second floor and quickly searched for any sign of the woman. He looked out of a window and could see lights coming on as dusk was setting. He needed to find the woman quickly before the town's gates were closed.

He listened at each door before opening it. The first three rooms were empty, he heard the sound of a couple lovemaking in the fourth and no sound in the fifth. He opened the door and peered in. He entered the room and there, tied up on the floor, was a body. He knelt down and could make out the shallow breathing of the woman. She had blond hair and the cloak she was wrapped in was brown. He picked her up in his arms and carried her back to the stairs.

He stopped and listened and then carried her down the stairs and out of the back door and into the stables. Owain went out to the street and waved for Huw to join him.

The big man entered the stables, joining Owain in a stall where he had put the unconscious woman. He peeled back the cloak and saw the ruined dress on the woman's body, covered in blood from a series of small cuts on her chest and abdomen.

"She needs medical help," said Owain. "Can you get her to the abbey on your own?"

"Yes, but what are you going to do?" asked Huw, concerned for his nephew.

"Get the bastard who did this," said Owain with more force than he intended.

"Better leave him, don't just go after him because of this." Huw looked down on the woman and sighed. "Keep your head. Gaspard has got more men than us and if we free the woman that's what we said we would do. We've kept our promise to Will."

"You forget he shot Caradoc and now this. The man's an animal; he has to be stopped before he kills anyone else." Owain turned away and walked back into the inn.

There was a hand cart at the back of the stable so Huw pulled it out, lifted the injured woman into the cart and covered her with some horse blankets. He got between the shafts of the cart and with a great jerk started it rolling. He pulled it out of the stable and into the street.

It was not that far to the Benedictine abbey church of St Peter and St Paul. When he arrived at the gate Huw pulled up the cowl of his cloak and masked his face before he knocked on the door of the abbey.

Shrewsbury Abbey

Huw did not have to wait long before a monk opened the small window and asked his business. Huw rapped on the door again and the monk got the message and opened the gate. Huw pulled the cart through the gate and dropped the shafts. He went to the rear of the cart and uncovered the woman.

"She's been tortured and is in need of help," said Huw.

The monk pulled back the cloak and stepped back in horror at the woman's wounds. "Who did this?" the monk demanded.

"I think you should get someone to care for her rather than looking at me with your accusing eyes, monk. This was not my work. Where is your infirmarian?" Huw said as he helped Kate to get up from the cart.

"Brother Michael is in the chapel. I'll go and get him but we have no facilities to care for a woman."

The monk ran off and returned within a few minutes with the prior and the infirmarian. The prior was a thin gaunt man who peered at the woman as if she was a creature from another world.

The infirmarian pulled away the cloak and the dress and inspected the wounds. He wiped away the blood and looked with disgust at the pattern of cuts on the woman's torso.

He looked up at Huw and said, "Who did this?"

"I found her like that and I know her husband and will send for him. Can you heal her?"

The prior interrupted. "We cannot take her in without knowing what has happened to her."

Huw drew himself up to his full height and looked down at the thin little man before him. "This woman needs your help. This was not done by me or by her husband, and the man who did it will be punished, I promise you, but all I ask of you is to tend her wounds and keep her safe until her husband can collect her. Didn't your Christ do as much for a Samaritan?"

Huw glared into the prior's eyes.

Brother Michael broke the tension by saying, "We can put her in the small shed in the herb garden." He turned to Huw and asked, "Can you carry her there?"

Huw scooped the woman up into his arms and followed the infirmarian through the dark grounds of the abbey. The infirmarian led the big man through the herb garden and down a narrow path to a small potting shed.

The monk pushed open the door and Huw entered. He put the woman down on a pallet next to the wall. He straightened up. "Her husband will ask for his wife by name, that way you'll know you have the right man."

"What is her name?"

"Her husband will know and if she's awake she'll recognise him," said Huw. "Just take good care of her. Remember, I know where you are."

"There's no need for threats. I will take care of her but she has so many small cuts and I think she's been drugged, but hopefully that will wear off. I think you should leave now."

"I'll leave the blankets that were in the cart but I need to take the cart back to where I borrowed it from."

Brother Michael guided Huw back to the gatehouse where the prior and the other monk were waiting. Huw pulled some coins from his pouch and took hold of the prior's hand. He placed the coins into the hand and folded it closed. Huw squeezed the prior's hand and the man screamed in pain as his face blanched.

"Be sure you take good care of my friend's wife or I will return with a wrath the like of which your god has not seen."

Huw tossed the blankets out of the cart and picked up the shafts and steered the cart out of the gate. The monk was about to close the gate behind him when the prior stopped him. He stepped out of the gate and watched the big man walk away until he was out of sight. The immense size of the man was impressed on the prior's memory; he was not the sort of man to forgive or to forget. He went back though the gate and said to the other monk, "Have those taken to the laundry and have them washed. Go and see Brother Michael and find out the woman's condition and tell me how she is."

The monk picked up two of the blankets and was about to leave when the prior said, "Make sure that you keep a record of what the infirmarian spends on this woman. And make sure he has one of his apprentices with her at all times. I want to know everything. When the husband arrives bring him to me for questioning before he sees the woman."

The monk nodded his understanding and left to find a novice.

Huw pushed the cart back to The Lion inn and put it back where he had found it in the corner of the stables. He waited in the shadows for any sign of Ednyfed. After a few minutes he thought about entering the inn. He went out from the stables into the street and looked up and down but the street was clear. He walked back towards the centre of town and had not gone more than thirty yards when a hand reached out and pulled him into a narrow alley.

He had his dagger half drawn when he saw who was pulling him into the alley. Iolo whispered, "The town guard have been round and I don't think we'll get him tonight because he's still with a group of his men."

"Where are the others?"

"Ednyfed and Owain are still in the inn. I sent Dafydd back to Frankwell to prepare the men so they will be ready to leave in a hurry."

"We have to take him tonight before he raises the alarm that we've taken the woman. Maybe one of us should be waiting in the dormitory for him?"

"I'll go and let Owain know you're back. I'll come out to the privy and let you know the plan." Iolo slipped away into the street and made his way to the front of The Lion.

Huw walked back to the stables, he moved from doorway to doorway, making sure he wasn't seen. He kept to the shadows and was soon back in the shadows within the stable. He checked the horses in the stables and saw that there were some fine mounts. He slipped halters on five of the horses and prepared a fire with hay and twigs. A fire was always a good distraction in a town where many of the buildings were wooden and the streets were so narrow. Town dwellers were always terrified of fire.

He was just putting some finishing touches to his fire when he heard a footfall. He stepped into the shadows and hid behind the stall of the horse he most wanted to take with him.

A man stepped into the barn and looked around. From his movements Huw could tell he was the worse for drink. The man stood in the middle of the stables and started to count the horses. He swayed unsteadily and staggered out of the stables in the direction of the privy. Once he had gone Huw heard a stream of urine being expelled from the man's bladder. There was an audible sigh of relief as the man came back from the privy. Huw stepped out and hit the man hard on the jaw and he collapsed like a sack of turnips. Huw found some twine and bound the man hand and foot. He gagged him with some rags and carried him to the back of the barn and dropped him on some straw, then threw some loose hay over the man and left him unconscious.

As he returned to his listening post at the front of the barn he heard Owain whispering, "Huw, Huw, where are you?"

Huw stepped out of the shadows, "Over here."

Owain and Huw moved to the back of the stables. "What were you doing?"

"Checking out the horse flesh and catching a drunk."

"What if he's missed?"

"The state he was in they'll think he's just gone to sleep it off somewhere."

"Gaspard's still with half a dozen of his men, so we'll just have to wait." Owain paused and had an intriguing thought, "Can you carry this drunk of yours?"

"I suppose so, why do you want him?"

"Let's wrap him in a cloak and put him in the room where I found Will's wife. That way when Gaspard goes to his room there will be a body there, which is exactly what he's expecting."

Huw smiled. "What if I were the body wrapped in the cloak?"

"Good idea, let's go."

Owain guided Huw to the room where he had found Kate. Huw lay down and Owain positioned him in the way he had found the tortured woman. Owain returned to the bar room and told Ednyfed what Huw had planned for Gaspard.

Ednyfed sent Iolo back to Frankwell to make sure the men were all ready to leave Shrewsbury as soon as they got the word from him.

Ednyfed and Owain watched as Gaspard and his men got drunker and soon the landlord was encouraging them to make use of the beds upstairs. Their rowdy behaviour was making other customers nervous and some of the regulars had already slipped out of the inn. The landlord did not like having soldiers in his inn as they disturbed the townsfolk who were his best customers and he didn't want to lose the local trade. On the other hand he couldn't say no to a powerful marcher lord like Lord de Grey.

Slowly, one by one the men went to their beds until only Gaspard and three others were left. Owain wanted to make a move but Ednyfed made him wait. Eventually Gaspard struggled to his feet and headed for the door. He made a drunken dash for the privy. He returned to the inn and struggled to climb the stairs. Owain followed him at a discrete distance.

Gaspard entered his room and staggered to his bed. He leaned over and prodded the body on the floor and was terrified when the body of the woman rose up and grabbed him by the throat. He tried to defend himself but the apparition before him was far too strong. Huw lifted Gaspard off the ground by the grip he had on Gaspard's throat.

With a mighty blow to the head Huw knocked Gaspard unconscious. He threw the body across his shoulders, opened the door and peered out. The hall was empty.

Owain waved to him from the stairs and he moved silently down the corridor and down the stairs. Huw made straight for the stables while Owain covered his retreat. Owain returned to the bar and he and Ednyfed left the inn by the door leading to the street.

When they got to the stables Huw had Gaspard secured on a horse tied across a saddle and was in the process of saddling another horse for himself. Owain and Ednyfed followed his lead. As soon as Huw had his horse saddled he got out his tinder box and started to light the fire he had set earlier.

"What do you think you're doing?" demanded Ednyfed.

"Creating a little diversion to cover our escape." He struck the flint and steel and a spark ignited the dry straw. Huw fanned the flames, and as soon as there was a good flame he gathered the lead reins on the horses and led them out of the stables into the street. He mounted and set off eastwards for the town gate. Ednyfed and Owain followed. They stopped at the end of the street and waited for the flames to attract someone's attention. They waited with growing impatience but they all knew that if they ran too early they could be caught by the town guard.

Iolo came running along the street and when he got to the inn he saw the flames coming from the stables. He shouted "Fire! Fire!" as loud as he could.

Some guards came running along the street and the landlord ran from the inn. Soon the street was filled with people all trying to put the fire out. A fire in a town crowded with wooden buildings could spell disaster, so everyone rushed to help put the fire out. The number of people caused confusion as there was no real leadership but somehow buckets were found and water thrown onto the burgeoning fire.

The three horsemen walked their mounts slowly to the gate. The gatekeeper looked up at the three men and said, "You can't leave now, it's gone dusk. There's a curfew, you know."

As he spoke Owain kicked him in the jaw, sending him sprawling in the mud. Owain was on him before he could get to his feet. He hit the gatekeeper hard behind the ear with the hilt of his dagger and the man sagged to the ground, unconscious. Owain opened the gate and they led the horses out, then he secured the gate and ran to join them.

They rode west, trusting that Iolo would return to Frankwell and lead the rest of the men back to the border.

"Where are we heading for?" asked Huw as they trotted along the road.

"We'll circle round the town and head towards Montgomery. We can go to Dolforwyn and back along the valley to the hill fort. Once we're clear of the town we'll slow down so Iolo and the others can catch up. And we need to send someone to tell Will where to find his wife."

They rode steadily round the town and forded the Severn, swimming the horses across. Once they were on the Welsh side of the river Huw nudged the unconscious body but the man was still dead to the world.

Severn Valley

Once he had raised the alarm Iolo slipped quietly away through the crowd. He walked through dark streets of the town and instead of trying to cross the Norman bridge he went down to the riverside and waded into the river and swam across to the western side. When he arrived at The Buck inn most of the men were asleep in the bar. He woke Dafydd and set him to wake the others while he spoke to the landlord. Dafydd sent men to saddle all the horses and to get William up and onto his horse. Iolo got the landlord to prepare some food for the journey and paid him well. The landlord, who was a Welshman, knew Iolo and was happy to oblige.

The men were soon in the saddle and heading west for Offa's Dyke and the Welsh border. Iolo took the lead so he could set a good pace. He designated two men to guard William, Lord de Grey's archer, who they still had as a hostage. The spare horses were distributed between the other riders. They made their way through the dark streets of Frankwell but there were no town guards to stop them and they were well on their way before dawn broke over the town.

As the sun came up Dafydd took over the lead as Iolo sagged in his saddle from fatigue of his activities in the night. They made good time as they didn't have to cross the river and were soon miles away from the Shrewsbury where the fire was still raging in the narrow streets of the town. Dafydd looked back and could see the smoke still billowing above the town.

They rode along the Severn Valley towards Welshpool. Iolo knew Ednyfed would go straight west as soon as he got out of Shrewsbury, so Iolo led the rest of the raiding party by the easiest route for the border before the English realised what had happened. He wanted to be well clear of Shrewsbury before it was discovered that Gaspard had been taken prisoner.

The two groups found each other at dawn just below the castle at Dolforwyn where the river Mule flows into the fast flowing Severn. They met at the junction between the two rivers and the whole party moved south-west following the river Mule up a narrow valley towards the Vale of Ceri.

The men were very tired and many of them were visibly sagging in their saddles after their long rides. Ednyfed knew he wanted to keep his two captives in a secure place until he could question them but he also wanted to hold them in separate places so they could not talk to each other. He wanted to test Gaspard's story against William's.

He took them to the old hill fort between Llanmerwig and Ceri. The fort had not been used for many years but Ednyfed used it occasionally as a sheep fold. He sent Owain and Huw ahead to prepare for their arrival. Huw put up a lean-to on the western side of the small round fort and Owain cleaned out the shelter some shepherds used to the north of the enclosure. Just to the south of the fort there was a small wood where two men were sent to collect firewood.

They were just starting a fire when the main group arrived. Ednyfed had Gaspard taken to the shelter and William was taken to the small lean-to. Once the prisoners were secure Ednyfed set a guard and told his men to get some rest.

Ednyfed sent Dafydd back to his farm, which was higher up the valley, to bring food. Huw and Owain sat by their small fire and Ednyfed joined them.

"We need a rider to tell Will about his wife, and we need to have guards for the prisoners."

"What are you going to do with the extra horses we brought back?" asked Huw, looking at the extra horses in the picket line.

"Send them south where they won't be recognised," suggested Owain.

"No, they go to Lord Rhys the other side of Caersws, he breeds horses," said Ednyfed. "He will appease the other lords of Powys on our behalf."

Owain, recognising the name, volunteered, "I'll take them over there once I've had some sleep. The sooner they are gone from here the better."

Ednyfed nodded his agreement. "Iolo and Huw can go to see Will and guide him to the abbey at Shrewsbury if needed. I'll keep some men here but the others can go to their homes and just return to act as guards as we need them."

"What about Caradoc?" asked Owain. "I'm sure he'll want to meet these two face to face."

"You two stay here. I'm going to the farm to see how Caradoc is doing. I'll be back before noon."

Owain rolled into his blanket and Huw stood up and started to walk round the perimeter of the little earthwork. Ednyfed rode along the track to the south of the fort, round the wood and up the hill to his farm. He climbed slowly toward the farm just below the motte which guarded the hill above the town of Newtown which was laid out on the valley floor in the oxbow of the Severn.

———————

The lone rider left Frankwell when he heard the commotion caused by Ednyfed's men. He saw the smoke rising above the town and knew that it was time to return and report to his master. He thought about going into the town but dismissed the idea when he saw flames rising above the buildings. He decided that not being in Shrewsbury was a good idea.

His horse was tired after his ride from Ludlow so he set a steady pace, taking a direct route through the impenetrable forest that stretched along the Marches. He knew that if he kept a steady pace he could get back to his master before the raiding party could go to ground.

As he rode west he could see the tracks of the men he was following in the moonlight. He stopped and cut some branches to use as a brush and he dragged them along behind him, wiping the tracks from the road.

While his master would want to know what was going on he did not think he would want the raiders captured by Lord de Grey.

Shrewsbury

The town guard was in disarray as they fought the fire which had started in the stables of The Lion Inn. It would have been much worse if someone hadn't raised the alarm but now, in the cold light of day, the damage to the street could be seen. The inn was still standing but the stables were completely destroyed and two other buildings had been burned to the ground. There were men and animals missing.

A sergeant of the guard was talking to the landlord to determine how many people were sleeping upstairs in the inn when Lord de Grey rode up. He was concerned about the number of men he had lost. First Jorge's patrol had disappeared, then the two men Gaspard had sent to collect the rope on the escarpment had not yet arrived in the town and now an inn where some of his men were billeted had been burned down. This run of bad luck was more than a coincidence; something was going wrong and he was determined to get to the bottom of it.

Lord de Grey looked round for Gaspard but could not see him. He rode along the street but still couldn't see his sergeant. He called all his men to him and he counted seven where there should have been at least ten or more.

"Where's Gaspard?" he demanded.

"I haven't seen him this morning, my lord," replied Eric, one of his men of Saxon decent shown by the blondness of his hair.

"How many horses were in those stables?"

"About ten or eleven of them, my lord, but the wagons were parked in the park near the abbey. We've lost ten horses and our oxen. We haven't found all the bodies yet. It's possible they won't be found, because the fire was so fierce."

"Eric, you take over as sergeant until we find Gaspard. Get the men together and find out just how many horses we have left. If we need more horses, let me know." Lord de Grey turned his horse back in the direction of the castle. He twisted in the saddle. "I don't suppose there's been any sign of Jorge yet?"

"No, my lord," said Eric, who was thinking about how he could make his promotion permanent.

"Ask around, see if you can find out any thing. You might try over in Frankwell."

Lord de Grey rode off in the direction of the castle. Eric looked at the men he had left and started organising them into groups. He wanted quick results so that he could keep his temporary promotion.

"Does anyone speak Welsh?" he asked the group.

Two men put their hands up and Eric said, "You're with me."

He sent one men to check on the wagons and two others to find horses and he left one to search through the inn for their equipment and to be there if any more men turned up. Although he suspected they were dead.

Eric led the way through the streets to the Welsh bridge. He knocked on the door of the guardhouse and asked the guard about the people who had entered the town that morning and the previous day.

The guard at the bridge said that there were few people who had entered the town that morning but there were a number of men who had entered the town from Frankwell the previous day. Eric set out to have his men check each of the inns to ask about any men who were not in the town on normal business.

Eric told David, one of his Welsh speakers, to stay with him and he told the other man, Rhys, to hang back and listen to any conversations while he and David questioned the innkeepers.

They started at the inns nearest the bridge and asked each innkeeper about the customers they had had over the last few days. It was lunchtime by the time they got to The Buck tavern.

Eric talked to the innkeeper about his guests but got no information. When he got outside the inn, Rhys guided him away, saying, "One of the guests told me that there were a group of Welshman here last night but they pulled out very early this morning, before dawn. The merchant was woken by their horses as they got ready to leave."

Rhys said, "I think we need another word with the landlord."

Eric stopped him by taking hold of his arm and holding him back.

"Wait a moment. We now know this innkeeper works with the Welsh so we can watch him. Did your merchant hear where these men were going?"

"He didn't say but there are only a few roads into Wales so we could follow their tracks," said Rhys, knowing that his lordship would want to take a ride in that direction.

"How many men were there?"

"At least a dozen from what the merchant said. He complained to the landlord but was told to go back to bed. He wasn't pleased and has been moaning about it all morning to the other guests and to anyone else who will listen."

Eric thought for a moment and said, "Find the merchant and tell him that it will be worth his while to take his complaint to Lord de Grey at the castle. If he objects we'll take him to see his lordship by force, but if you can get him to volunteer that would be so much better."

Rhys returned to the inn and was soon back with the merchant in tow. Eric led the way back over the Welsh bridge and to the castle where he got the guard to take them directly to Lord de Grey.

Lord de Grey came striding out of the gatehouse. "What have you got then, Eric?"

"This man says a party of Welshmen rode from The Buck inn in Frankwell just about the time the fire started at the stables of The Lion inn. That seems very suspicious to me. What's more, the innkeeper didn't mention it when we asked him about any new travellers in the town."

Lord de Grey turned to the merchant. "Tell me everything you saw and heard and leave nothing out."

The merchant muttered something under his breath and stuttered, "I didn't actually see anything, it was too dark, but there was a lot of noise after midnight, it woke me up. I heard men bringing horses out into the road and then they rode off to the west. The inn was empty this morning where there had been at least a dozen men there the evening past."

"They would have to go west because the river is to the east and south," said Eric. "What else did you hear?"

"When I was in the bar earlier there were three men who had another man who seemed to be their prisoner. They had him cornered in a booth," the merchant said.

"Describe him."

"Slightly above average height. Older than me, maybe thirty-five to forty." The merchant closed his eyes to visualise the man. "He had colours under his cloak, blue and white, I think. The same as those on your shield." He pointed to the shield attached to Lord de Grey's saddle.

"William or Jared by the sound of it and it would explain why they haven't turned up in Shrewsbury yet," said Eric, trying to impress his lordship.

"William. Jared's just a boy. But who would dare to hold him prisoner? Gaspard has a lot to answer for when I find him." Lord de Grey was angry at the trouble his sergeant was putting him to; he should have been back at his huge red castle in Ruthin days ago but here he was wasting time in Shrewsbury trying to find his men, or what was left of them.

"Eric, gather all the men together. I think we need to take a look to the west to see what is going on," said the lord. "And bring him with you." He pointed at the merchant. The merchant started to protest but a look from Eric silenced him, although he let the man slip away as he didn't want to be lumbered with an extra person look after, especially on a raid into a wilder part of Wales.

"Meet me here at the castle in an hour." Lord de Grey strode off as he wanted to talk with the other marcher lords before he had a foray into Wales. He wanted the other lords as allies, not enemies, and he knew he may need their help. He only wished he could draw some men and supplies from his estates in Kent but he felt he needed to take action now. He was pleased with Eric; the man was proving his worth and he would make a good sergeant now it appeared that he had lost Jorge and Gaspard was missing.

Newtown

The tired horseman arrived at the edge of the town and wondered if Lord Rhys was in the town or at his estates further west. He had ridden through the night and had overtaken Iolo and his men as they struggled to keep their group together. He stabled his horse and went on a tour of the inns to find the lord or any of his men.

Gwyn Mochyn finally found Tegwyn, Lord Rhys's steward, in The Checkers inn on the broad street of Newtown. Gwyn walked into the inn and tapped Tegwyn on the shoulder. Tegwyn had been drinking but was not drunk. He turned and had his sword half out of its scabbard before he realised who he was facing.

"If that sword comes clear, you're a dead man," came Gwyn's stern warning, his hand resting on his dagger. Tegwyn slid the sword back and looked into Gwyn Mochyn's tired eyes. "What do you want?"

"To know where Lord Rhys is because I have some news for him and I think he'd rather hear it sooner than later. We could have serious trouble if he doesn't take some action and I've ridden all night to find him."

"As luck would have it his lordship is upstairs. I'll go and get him. Wait here."

Tegwyn left the bar and went up to the room which was kept for Lord Rhys's private use. The lord was listening to a monk reading back a letter he had just composed when Tegwyn entered the room.

"Gwyn Mochyn's in the bar and I fear he has bad news from the other side of the border. He says he's ridden all night to find you."

"Bring him up here. I don't want any rumours spread unless I order it. And bring up some food and ale, he'll need it if he's been riding all night."

Within minutes Gwyn Mochyn was ushered into Lord Rhys's room. He slipped his cloak from his shoulders and dropped it on a chair by the door. Lord Rhys held up his hand as a signal that he should say nothing until the monk, who had been scribing for him, had left the room. The monk packed away his writing materials into a leather satchel and was about to leave when Lord Rhys said, "Don't go far, I may have need of you again when I have spoken to Gwyn."

The monk nodded his acquiescence and left the room. They waited until they heard the monk reach the bottom of the stairs. Rhys waved Gwyn towards the seat vacated by the monk.

"What is it that is so urgent you came looking for me in daylight?" demanded Lord Rhys indignantly.

Gwyn opened his satchel and pulled out the partially burned tabard and passed it over to the lord. He waited for Lord Rhys to inspect the garment.

"Ednyfed's men wiped out a party of men wearing tabards like that. They were Lord de Grey's men. I counted about ten of them," reported Gwyn.

"Damn, I warned him not to do anything stupid. This will mean reprisals and we aren't equipped to fight a lord like de Grey."

"There's more, it was Lord de Grey's men who shot young Caradoc and they were hunting him in Clun. The area between Clun and Ludlow was crawling with his men but Lord de Grey has moved to Shrewsbury from Ludlow two days ago."

"Good, maybe he's given up on the boy. Do you know why he wanted the boy dead?" asked Rhys. The more he knew the better he could deal with the coming situation.

There was a knock at the door and a serving girl entered with a tray. She put the tray on the table and left. Both men waited until they were sure she was out of earshot and then Gwyn continued. "It seems as if he thought the boy was carrying a message to someone. I don't think he wanted it delivered."

Gwyn poured himself some ale and took a good draught to wash the dust of the road from his throat. He set down the goblet and tore apart some bread and nibbled it.

"What's Ednyfed got himself into now?" asked Rhys rhetorically.

"I don't think the boy was the messenger, I think he was just in the wrong place at the wrong time," said Gwyn, pouring himself some more ale.

Lord Rhys stood up and poured himself a drink. "Then we'd better find this messenger. And quickly. Do you have any ideas who he could be?"

Gwyn put down his drink. "No, my lord, but there's something else you need to know. Ednyfed's men set light to something in Shrewsbury. I could see the smoke rising over the town from Frankwell. I don't know what it was but they left Frankwell in a hurry last night and I had a job to overtake them. I last saw them heading for Dolforwyn Castle."

"Why there?" mused Rhys and he walked to the door and shouted down the stairs, "Tegwyn, get up here now!"

Gwyn went to the top of the stairs and shouted, "Tegwyn!"

Tegwyn came running up the stairs and nearly slipped on the final step. He crashed into the wall and then straightened up, regaining his composure as he entered the room.

Lord Rhys gave him an amused look and said to Gwyn, "Tell him what you've just told me."

Gwyn told Tegwyn what he had told Lord Rhys and the steward tried to stifle his smile. "I told you if you left them they'd do something stupid, and I was right."

"I don't need stupid comments from you now, I need you to get as many men as you can muster and get them to the ford below Dolforwyn Castle, where the Mule meets the Severn. Gwyn, go and get some sleep and then I want you out on the road from Shrewsbury in three hours. We need to intercept Lord de Grey if he decides to follow Ednyfed. We can't afford for him to get himself killed chasing an old soldier like Ednyfed. If he's killed that will draw the attention of the king and it cost all of us."

Then Lord Rhys had second thoughts. "Gwyn, find out where Ednyfed is and then report back to me. I'll be with Tegwyn trying to avoid a full scale war."

Gwyn reached for the burned tabard but Lord Rhys picked it up and threw it on the fire. "I think that the less evidence there is the better, don't you?" Rhys continued, "Did you leave anything where you found this?"

"No," said Gwyn, "everything was buried, even the carcasses of the dead horses had been dragged from sight. With a few days' wind and rain no one will find anything at Black Hill."

"Good, then let's keep it that way. Now go and find Ednyfed for me."

Gwyn turned and went down the stairs.

"You don't really trust him, do you?" asked Tegwyn as soon as Gwyn was out of sight.

"Not really but he can be very useful and he's loyal to gold and silver, so make sure you pay him. Now send my squire up so I can get dressed."

Tegwyn shrugged and went down the stairs to rouse the men.

"Oh! And send the monk up. I need to send a letter to Mortimer to warn him about Grey."

An hour later Lord Rhys was leading his men east towards Dolforwyn Castle.

Vale of Ceri

When Gwyn Mochyn left Lord Rhys he went down to the bar and ordered some more food. He found a seat by the fire where he could dry out and relax. Five minutes later the food arrived – mutton stew with some course grained bread delivered by a maid who he would have chatted to if he hadn't been so tired. Gwyn attacked the first hot meal he'd had in days with relish, but as he did so he scanned the room, watching the men present. He noted the men in the common room as they observed him.

He noted each of the men he knew who worked for Lord Rhys and made a note of each of the others present. If he heard any gossip about himself he would be making a call to ensure their silence. He did not want his association with the lord bandied about.

Once he had finished his meal he threw his cloak around his shoulders and went to find a fresh horse. Within an hour he was back in the saddle, riding south up the steep hill towards the Vastre. He would make a call at Ednyfed's farm to enquire about the boy and to see if Ednyfed had returned from across the border.

He took his time climbing the steep slope because he didn't want to tire his new horse. The fresh horse was not as sturdy as his own horse and he did not want to wear it out at the start of his journey as he didn't know when he would need the older horse to run at speed. The ostler had not had a good selection of mounts, or perhaps he did not trust Gwyn with his better horses. *Terrible thing, a bad reputation,* he thought as he rode on.

By dusk he was sitting on the top of the Vastre looking down onto the farm on the slope below. There seemed little activity at the farm and he could not seen Ednyfed or Owain. Mags came out of the house to feed the stock but as soon as she had finished her chores she returned to the kitchen.

The southerly wind came up and Gwyn Mochyn pulled his cloak tighter around him. His perch was too exposed so he decided to get closer to the farm to get out of the wind and get warmer. He knew his view of the farm would not be as good but he wanted a little more comfort.

He dismounted and walked with his horse down to the small wood just to the south of the farm. Once there, he removed the saddle from the horse and hobbled her so she could graze. He found a suitable tree where he could rest his back and still see the farmyard clearly. He sat down with his saddle and his blanket and made himself comfortable. He wrapped his blanket round himself and prepared to watch and wait.

He soon dropped off to sleep and he didn't see the men coming and going from the farm. He slept soundly and only woke the following morning as the sun came up.

Shrewsbury –
Severn Valley – Montgomery Castle

An hour later Lord de Grey was waiting at the castle gate as Eric arrived with twenty men. They formed up into lines and half of them didn't have horses, having lost them in the fire at The Lion inn. The others were saddled and ready to ride.

Lord de Grey was not pleased. "Where are the rest of the men and where are their horses?"

"We lost ten horses when The Lion burned and Jorge had another dozen or so with him. We've still got the oxen and the wagons safe at the abbey," said Eric, seeing his master's face cloud over.

"I want to travel fast, not with the wagons, you idiot. I'll go and see how many horses we can borrow from the Talbots. You get the men who have horses ready and sort out the rest into those who can ride and those who can't. I need men who can ride and fight. Where is William?" Lord de Grey looked at his men and thought, *They don't seem that keen on a raid into Wales.* He counted the men and noted various men missing apart from Gaspard, William and Jared. Nothing seemed to have gone right since they'd arrived at Ludlow Castle.

Lord de Grey was back with a guide and six horses within half an hour. Eric picked five men and mounted a horse himself. He hadn't wanted to admit to Lord de Grey that his was one of the horses that had been lost in the fire at The Lion. Eric arranged for the rest of his men to stay with the wagons and to take care of the oxen and the heavier draught horses. The men who were staying in Shrewsbury were all given tasks to find out more about the Welshmen who visited the town and its fairs. Lord de Grey thought he knew the Welsh but he was learning that maybe he did not understand them as well as he thought he did.

He led his men over the Welsh bridge through Frankwell and onto the road west towards Welshpool as he wanted to avoid Montgomery. The great fortress there stood proud on a rocky premonitory overlooking the Severn Valley, the sheer walls of the cliff and the high stone walls making the castle a bastion against any invasion from the centre of Wales. He knew the castle was held by the Mortimers and he didn't want to have to explain his presence in Mortimer controlled territory.

They skirted round to the south of Welshpool and Lord de Grey followed the southern bank of the river Severn into the broad valley of the river. The road was a sea of mud after the previous days of rain and the men were not happy at taking this journey into Wales which was hostile to the incursions of the English. Their progress was slow and Lord de Grey had the men dismount to walk with their horses.

It was Eric who first noticed that they were being watched by some riders in the distance. He mounted and turned his horse from the party and rode towards the horsemen but they rode away. When he returned to Lord de Grey's troop, a horseman reappeared behind them. The men were all feeling nervous and it showed as their hands rested on their weapons. They all knew about Welsh bowmen and they hoped they would not find any. The further across the border they rode, the more nervous and jumpy they became.

They were all very cold and wet when they reached the Mule tributary just below Dolforwyn Castle. On the other side of the small river sat a group of horsemen. Lord de Grey rode forward and a man rode forward to meet him.

"Who are you?" demanded Lord de Grey.

"My name is Lord Rhys ap Hywel and I think you are a little out of your way, Lord de Grey," said Rhys in his rusty French.

"What do you mean?" demanded Lord Grey indignantly.

"Just that your lands are to the north and I don't think you have business here."

"Where I have business is none of yours. Now get your men out of my way or suffer the consequences."

Lord Rhys raised his arm and several archers appeared at the edge of a wood some forty yards away. Another group of archers appeared from behind a hedge near the river about thirty yards from Lord de Grey's men. Lord de Grey's men were caught on a killing ground between the two groups and in front of them was Lord Rhys with a troop of horsemen. The marcher lord looked about him and realised he must withdraw or lose most of his men. He was caught like a rat in a trap.

Lord Rhys rode forward to talk to the Lord de Grey without being overheard. "I am here because the Earl of Arundel and Sir Edmund Mortimer sent me to keep you from getting killed."

"Arundel, why?" That didn't make sense but he continued to listen.

"The Earl of Arundel doesn't want you dead and he doesn't want the king raging through his lands. That's why he sent me a message to escort you to Montgomery," lied Lord Rhys convincingly.

"Who do you think would want to kill me?" demanded the marcher lord.

"There's a man up on the hill with thirty men who has a son with an arrow through his shoulder. That man or his other son would kill you as soon as look at you. By the way, why did you shoot young Caradoc?" asked Lord Rhys with genuine curiosity.

"My sergeant Gaspard thought he was a messenger and if he had done his job there would have been no problem. He should have questioned the messenger and that would have been the end of it."

"I think you underestimate both the boy and his father," said Lord Rhys as he sat on his horse which was getting restless with the rain falling more heavily now. "I suggest we take shelter at Montgomery Castle. You can spend the night there before you return north."

"That's a long way off," Lord de Grey snapped as he felt the rain running down his face. The man sitting in front of him made no comment but just looked around at his men. Lord de Grey read his inference. He called Eric over to his side.

"We're going to Montgomery Castle for the night."

"Very good, my lord," said Eric with some relief, as he knew this would be popular with the men. He turned his horse and got the men moving into line to ride south-east toward Bryn Derwen Motte and on to Montgomery Castle.

"I'll ride with you, if I may?" said Lord Rhys, the question being rhetorical. Lord de Grey did not want the man's company but knew he had no option. He nodded his ascent and they rode side by side through the pouring rain.

Lord Rhys's men rode on the flanks of Lord de Grey's men, forming a protective screen. Lord de Grey noticed this and asked, "Who is this Caradoc and his father?"

"They are farmers and bowmen, and they have a large family in Montgomeryshire and Radnorshire. I know the father and several of the boy's uncles but I don't know Caradoc, the boy himself. Apparently he was travelling back home having visited an uncle in Oxford when he was shot. I believe the uncle is a monk at the Oxford priory. Shooting the boy hasn't made you popular, to say the least."

"Does this man know a lawyer named Owain Glyn Dwr?" Lord de Grey asked.

"I don't know, but I do know that Ednyfed took a party of men over the border to retrieve Caradoc's pack. They are *not* a forgiving family and they'll want revenge for your wounding the boy," warned Rhys sternly.

"Could the boy have been a messenger?" Lord de Grey probed again.

"He might have carried a message for his father or maybe the Mortimers, though I doubt it. I'm told he was considering becoming a monk, hence the reason for visiting his uncle at the abbey in Oxford."

Rhys could now see what had happened. Caradoc had been mistaken for a messenger to Glyn Dwr and Lord de Grey had some enmity toward the Welsh lawyer who had been an esquire to the king. To stop the message Lord de Grey had decided to stop the messenger but his men had stopped the wrong man.

"It sounds like you got the wrong man," mused Lord Rhys.

The journey to Montgomery Castle took over an hour by which time all of the men were soaked to the skin and feeling thoroughly miserable. Lord Rhys rode forward ahead of the men and spoke to the guard, who opened Arthur's Gate to let them into the small town. There was a solid rampart round the small town at the base of the high ridge.

Lord Rhys led the way up through the town to the castle gatehouse. The men were all shown to the stables and the barracks while Lord Rhys led Lord de Grey through the castle to the inner bailey. They had to pass through the heavily protected inner gate to get to the hall of the castle. Lord de Grey was impressed by the defences and how well the castle was built. The inner bailey and keep were nigh on impregnable.

Lord Rhys removed his cloak and followed the escorting guard into the hall where they found Sir Edmund Mortimer standing before a large fire. He turned and took in the two bedraggled men. "So you found him, Lord Rhys, I thank you."

Lord Rhys walked forward and stood before the fire to dry off. Reginald de Grey followed him, dropping his sodden cloak on a bench. So this Rhys really was a Welsh lord working with the marcher family. As the warmth seeped into the two wet travellers, Sir Edmund considered what he should do with them. He would send Lord Rhys home in the morning and then have more serious words with de Grey.

"Why have you had me brought here?" asked Lord de Grey as he held his hands out to the fire.

"Because I didn't want you dead and the border's ripe for rebellion. Archbishop Arundel has warned the king but he has troubles elsewhere with Scotland and that rebellion by Richard's supporters trying to put my nephew Edmund on the throne."

"King Henry's too good a soldier to be beaten by a few disgruntled old men. Look at his campaigns in Prussia. Richard is certainly no match for him and the king has him safely locked away in his castle at Pontefract," intimated Lord de Grey to his host.

"But at Vilnya he had a clear enemy to attack; here he is beset on all sides with men who will not just attack him man to man on the battlefield. And I can understand the Welsh point of view to a certain extent as he gives Welsh lands to Englishmen. It takes a lot to hold lands in Wales and the Welsh won't go away. You can hunt them down but they just fade away into their hills, isn't that so, Rhys?"

This was a dig at Lord de Grey who Sir Edmund knew had been involved in various disputes over land, and one in particular with a Welsh lord, Owain Glyn Dwr.

Lord Rhys nodded. "If you go after Caradoc and his father, Ednyfed, he will call on all his friends and relatives to attack not just you but any Englishman who has taken land in Wales. That includes any Englishman who is just travelling about his business in Wales. King Henry should know better because he holds land at Brecon from his de Bohun wife, does he not?"

Sir Edmund shouted for his servant and food was brought in and laid on the table near the fire. Wine was poured and the servants scurried out, leaving the three men alone in the hall. Sir Edmund sat down and started to eat. Lord de Grey and Lord Rhys joined him, suddenly realising how hungry they were after their journey through the saturating rain.

As their hunger subsided they continued their discussion. Sir Edmund led the talk. "The only way we can be prosperous is to keep the peace. Wars and never-ending raiding are expensive. If we can keep the peace and encourage trade then the richer we will all be. If we have war then the tenants can't harvest their crops, can't pay their rents and they starve and we will end up with no one to work the land. It's a vicious circle."

Lord de Grey answered, "The only way I can be prosperous is to enforce the rents from the lands I hold, and as you say, it's expensive to keep a force of armed men but I can see no option. I would rather deal with my tenants from a position of strength. Not only that, but the king demands that we provide him with troops for his wars with those who would depose him. So I can see no other way but to maintain a force of knights and men-at-arms."

"I understand what you are saying but if you were to employ more Welshmen in your army and treat them fairly they would take care of dealing with your tenants. Not only that, there are some very good bowmen in Wales. They are used to shooting longer distances because of the Welsh countryside. On the king's last foray to Scotland it was only his Welshmen who left the field in good order after the English were beaten," said Lord Rhys.

Lord de Grey didn't like the criticism of the English army although he knew it was true. He looked at the Welshman and rudely asked, "Just who are you?"

Sir Edmund answered, "Forgive me, this is Lord Rhys who holds land in the west of Montgomeryshire. I know no Englishman could hold it because all his animals would disappear into those dense forests and up into the mountains. However, Rhys understands that peace will serve us better than war. I use him as a sounding board for what is happening in Montgomeryshire. If I tried to enforce my rights through force I would have trouble because the Welsh would just ignore me and that would undermine my authority. By working with Rhys I am able to achieve more than I would otherwise. Lord Rhys's family have worked with the Mortimers for some time and we have an understanding."

Sir Edmund turned to face Lord de Grey. "Perhaps you would like to tell us about why you shot the boy, Caradoc, who was coming back from Oxford?"

"It appears to have been a mistake, Gaspard, my sergeant, thought the young man was a messenger but from what Rhys says he may have been just a traveller in the wrong place at the wrong time. Is the boy alive?"

"Yes, he's alive," answered Rhys curtly. "But I don't know how badly he's wounded. His father is very angry and I think he's been across the border to collect the boy's pack, among other things. I think they will have been asking questions about who was in the area when the boy was shot."

"What are the likely repercussions?" asked Sir Edmund, concerned about cross-border raids into his lands.

"Well, if Lord Grey goes north then I think they will leave it be. My bailiff had a man travel with Ednyfed. He told me that they killed all of Jorge's men just to the east of Black Hill which is to the east of Clun on the way to Ludlow. They ambushed him in a valley and killed all his men before interrogating Jorge. I'm told the fight lasted less than five minutes."

"What did your man do?" demanded Lord Grey, who was enraged to hear that Jorge and his men had been killed.

"Nothing, he was part of the raiding party. He also told me that one of your men took away a farmer's wife." Rhys left that hanging in the air.

Lord Grey looked confused. "A farmer's wife? What are you talking about?"

"A farmer's wife came to Ludlow with information for Jorge. He promised her a reward for information about the wounded boy. When Ednyfed met her husband he told him that she had been taken away by your men. Paul said they found her in an inn in Shrewsbury. And she'd been very badly treated – burns and cuts and more."

"Who was the farmer?" asked Sir Edmund.

"A man named Will. He lives between Ludlow and Clun. He could be one of your tenants," said Rhys, looking at Sir Edmund. When Sir Edmund said nothing he returned his attention to Lord de Grey's face for any sign of recognition.

Sir Edmund broke the silence. "I think I know the one; married a blonde girl from the midlands. He's a solid man and a good farmer, always pays his rent on time."

"So she was the reason Jorge charged off to Clun. I didn't know," said Lord de Grey. "Do you know where Gaspard is? He's my senior sergeant."

"Paul said that Ednyfed has two captives: an archer who they found on the ridge where Caradoc was shot and another, a man taken in Shrewsbury," Rhys admitted.

"What chance is there of getting them back?" Lord de Grey asked.

"Very little. I think I've already lost enough by delivering you to Sir Edmund. I don't think they will last very long if the boy identifies them as his assailants. If the boy dies then I think you can assume they will also be dead shortly after."

Sir Edmund looked thoughtful. "Couldn't you talk to the father? Make him see reason?"

"And say what? Can I have the men who tried to kill your son?" retorted the Welshman.

Lord de Grey noted Rhys's sarcasm. He was not used to being spoken to like this. The Welshman sat back in his chair and took a sip of his wine as if he was awaiting an onslaught from the English lord. When none came he continued.

"I think the best thing I can do is go and talk to Ednyfed but I need you and your men to be back on the other side of the border first. I think Gaspard is dead even if he's still breathing. I'll try to get the archer, but I make no promises."

Rhys didn't want to promise anything he couldn't deliver. He knew Ednyfed would kill both men instantly if he was threatened and that would not be good in the current climate with the new king still feeling unsafe on the throne and the marcher lords more or less free to do as they pleased in the Welsh Marches. The deposed King Richard still had conspirators who were plotting Henry's downfall and King Henry had more to think about than minor disputes in Wales, even if they did involve a good friend of his like Lord Reginald de Grey.

Sir Edmund drained his goblet and looked at the two men in front of him. "Reginald, you take your men and go home to Ruthin. There's nothing here for you but grief, and if you have grief I'll have more. Rhys, you go and talk to Ednyfed and tell him I want to meet him. Tell him I want his prisoners and that I know he has Gaspard and an archer. Tell him I'll listen to what he has to say but my word is the law."

"Do that and he'll kill them just to show his independence. Let me talk to him and let me talk to the boy. What can I offer them? The boy went to see his uncle who's a monk. Can I offer him a place at a monastery? Strata Florida?"

Sir Edmund nodded. "I'll think on it and talk to you about it in the morning. I'm for my bed. My servants will make you comfortable for the night. I'll see you in the morning."

Sir Edmund left the two men in the hall and retired to his bed chamber.

Reginald stood up and took off the remainder of his armour and wet clothes and wrapped himself in a dry blanket, towelling himself to get warm. Rhys opened the baggage one of the servants had delivered and changed into a fresh shirt and leggings. The two men settled down on benches ready for sleep.

"You really think this Ednyfed is a match for our forces?" Lord Grey asked, sure that his forces were too strong for any Welsh peasant.

"He wouldn't have to be, he'd just run you ragged all over the mountains of mid Wales and he would pick where to fight just as he did with Jorge. He would nibble away at the fringes of any army that came after him. There wouldn't be any pitched battles or major sieges. It would be a war of attrition. He would kill a man here and a horse there. He would get your men fighting against each other and burn your crops and hit your tenants so they would revolt because they were starving. I wouldn't underestimate him."

Rhys continued, "I know him, he fought beside me in France. He and his brothers are excellent bowmen and other men will follow them. What's more, they have had enough of English lords riding roughshod over our laws and traditions. He had plenty of support for his ride over the border."

"I'll go back to Shrewsbury tomorrow but I will keep an eye on what happens here. If he kills Gaspard I will come back," said Lord de Grey emphatically.

Rhys faced him angrily and said, "As I said, I will talk to Ednyfed but I can't guarantee that he will hand either of them over. What do I have to bargain with? A possible place in a monastery for Caradoc, which he would probably have got anyway. Maybe I should have let you find Ednyfed?"

Lord de Grey lay down but did not immediately go to sleep. He lay there thinking about how easily Rhys's men had surrounded him near the river. He had no archers with him and the Welshmen would have cut him to pieces at will. He had heard the stories about Crecy when the French had been cut to pieces by English archers with their bows. He would need to plan better next time he decided to venture into the wilder parts of Wales; certainly men—at—arms alone could not take this country without the support of bowmen. As it was the English only held parts of the country because of the huge fortresses they had built. The garrisons were expensive to maintain but Edward's castles were what really controlled the country.

However, Grey was under no illusion that away from the castles and the fortified towns that surrounded them that the countryside was controlled by the Welsh and it would take a huge army to fully subjugate this small hilly land.

Rhys was asleep as soon as he put his head down on his folded cloak.

Shrewsbury Abbey

Will went to the door of Shrewsbury Abbey and knocked. Iolo and Huw stayed back, watching from a distance. After what seemed a long time the small window opened in the door and a monk's face appeared. He stared at Will but said nothing.

"I was told that my wife is here. Her name is Kate," said Will anxiously.

The door swung open and the monk beckoned him in. The monk directed Will to a bench where he was left to wait.

Brother Michael, the infirmarian, arrived after an hour. He sat down next to Will. "I understand you've come for your wife?"

"That's right, where is she? Why have I been kept waiting so long?" said Will impatiently.

"Who told you she was here?" asked the monk.

Will ignored the question as he was feeling indignant at being kept waiting and asked what he thought were irrelevant questions.

"I don't think that's important. I have come to take Kate home," said the farmer.

"There is a young woman here but I can't just hand her over to anyone who arrives to take her away," said Brother Michael as he folded his hands into his lap.

"Then why don't you bring her here and she will recognise me. I will describe her for you. Kate has blonde hair and she is about half a hand shorter than me. She's twenty-two and we have been married for two years. We have a farm between Ludlow and Clun which I hold from the Mortimers. If you don't bring my wife to me, NOW, I'll complain to Sir Edmund Mortimer." Will stood up.

"No need for threats, I just have to know that giving her to you is in her best interests. Anyone could describe her; you could have got the description from the man who brought her here. And that was the night there was a serious fire in the town." Brother Michael said, "The Talbots are still trying to find out how it started."

Brother Michael had been instructed by the prior to find out who the woman was and why she had been delivered to the abbey, and if she had any connection to the fire that had caused so much damage in the town.

"She was kidnapped by one of Lord de Grey's men, and now I just want to take her home. The man who told me she was here told me she was badly used by Lord Grey. Now if you don't bring me my wife . . ."

"I don't think threats are appropriate. Let me talk to her and see if she recognises you." The monk realised that this was a delicate situation. Lord de Grey was not someone to cross and holding this man's wife could have other repercussions if she had been held against her will.

"Wait here and I will bring her to see you."

Will was about to protest but the monk was gone. He slumped back down on the bench to wait. He thought about following the monk through the inner door. He got up and tried it but found it locked.

Brother Michael went directly to the prior. He found him in the scriptorium reading a newly scribed document. "The woman's husband is here and he tells me that she was taken by Lord de Grey."

The name caught the prior's attention. "What else did you find out?"

"She's two-and-twenty and they've been married for two years. Her husband has a farm between Ludlow and Clun which means he's probably one of Mortimer's tenants. He said he would complain to Sir Edmund."

The prior sat down and thought on the dilemma. Did he go to the castle and find Lord de Grey and return the woman to him or could he let the farmer have her? If the farmer went to Sir Edmund that could be just as bad and he had closer ties with the Talbots who held the lordship of Shrewsbury.

"So we have a farmer who probably holds his land from the Mortimers and we have Lord de Grey of Ruthin. What do you think we should do?"

"Lord Grey left Shrewsbury two days ago going west towards Welshpool. I don't think he'll be back. From the talk in the town he's already lost one patrol of men who were searching for a wounded man around Clun."

"Where did you get that snippet of information?" asked the prior, intrigued at how the infirmarian could have such information when he had not left the abbey grounds for over a week.

"From the woman, Kate. She told me about how the earl's men were searching for a messenger and how they couldn't find him. She also said that a sergeant named Jorge had gone missing with eight or nine men-at-arms. She went to the castle to tell this Jorge about a man she saw on the road and that was when the other sergeant, Gaspard, took her and tortured her."

The prior was now enraged at Brother Michael. "Why didn't you tell me this as soon as she told you? We could have got rid of her sooner. She will only bring trouble down upon us."

Brother Michael could see the fear in the prior's eyes. He had never seen the man so scared. The prior was usually a bully but now he could see he was just a coward hiding behind his orders.

"The best thing to do, then, is to give her to her husband and send them on their way as soon as possible. If Lord Grey has gone hunting trouble in Wales he may very well not return and if he does he will probably just go home to Ruthin." Brother Michael stopped as a thought just hit him. "The woman has never once mentioned seeing Lord Grey. What if the sergeant took the woman for himself and just hid her in the wagon?"

"Get the woman and get her to identify her husband and the man who brought her here and then get rid of her. Quickly and quietly," said the prior, wanting to be rid of the problem before it got any worse.

"I'll do that," said the infirmarian, and he left the prior and went to find Kate in the infirmary. He found her doing some sewing, repairing the rents in her dress.

"A man has come for you. He says he's your husband."

Kate looked up at Brother Michael. Her stare was far away and he was not sure she had understood what he had said. Brother Michael took her hand gently and took away the needle she was holding. He helped her to her feet and she started to brush her skirts as if to make herself more presentable.

"Will is here?" she asked in a whisper.

"That's what he said his name was and he described you quite well. He said you've been married for two years and that you live on a farm near Ludlow. To the west of Ludlow towards Clun."

"Yes, that's right."

"Shall we go and see him?"

She nodded her ascent and rose to walk with the monk to the gatehouse. Brother Michael showed her into the room where Will was waiting, and she threw herself into her husband's arms. He held her close and they stood there for several moments. They slowly became aware of the monk and Kate turned to him.

"Brother Michael, this is my husband, Will."

"My blessings be upon you and I wish you a safe journey home," said the monk.

"Thank you for looking after her," said Will, who was keen to get away from the abbey as soon as he could.

Will opened the door and led Kate out into the cold of the afternoon. They walked away towards the town. Brother Michael watched them as they walked away and he was joined by the prior, whose curiosity had got the better of him.

"It was her husband. She was very pleased to see him from her reaction."

The prior said nothing but watched until the man and woman were out of sight.

They did not see Iolo watching them from further along the road.

Frankwell – West of Shrewsbury

As soon as they were in the town Will turned to Kate and said, "I told you that no good would come of talking to that Jorge, didn't I?"

"Yes, and you were right." She stood contrite but he knew it wouldn't last. He felt guilty for saying it but it had to be said so that it wouldn't happen again.

"We'll stay the night in Frankwell and go home tomorrow. I am now in the debt of some very dangerous Welshmen. They got you away from Lord de Grey's men and they took you to the abbey so you'd be safe. I beg you to do as I bid you in future or the outcome may not go as well."

They walked through the streets of Shrewsbury and Kate took much interest in the stalls with all their fine wares. Will bought her some material to make a new dress as the one she was wearing was so badly damaged. They did not notice Iolo or Huw as they followed them through the narrow streets of the town. Iolo made sure they were not followed. It was only when they reached The Buck inn that Will saw the two men as they entered the inn.

Will found Kate a seat at a table and then he invited the two Welshmen to join them. Kate recognised the huge man as the one who had carried her from the stables behind the inn where she had been held prisoner by Gaspard.

"I hope you are recovered from your ordeal, Mistress Kate," said Huw, seeing the recognition in her eyes.

"Yes, thank you."

Iolo ordered food and drink and they settled uncomfortably as a company.

Once the food arrived Iolo started to ask Kate gentle questions to get her talking. As soon as she was talking at ease he moved the conversation to what had happened at the castle.

"Did they treat you well at the castle in Ludlow?" he probed gently.

"The guard was fine and the sergeant Jorge just rushed away after he questioned me. The other sergeant . . . he's the one who tore my dress and . . ."

They could see where she had tried in vain to repair it. The answers Iolo wanted were not going to come while Will was sitting there next to her. He nudged Huw and indicated with a nod of his head towards the game on the other side of the room.

Huw stood up. "Come with me and let's have a look this game. Do you know the rules?"

Will got up uneasily and went across to explain the rules of the game to Huw.

Kate watched them go and then turned to see Iolo watching her intently. She finished her food and took a sip from her drink. Iolo mirrored her by taking a drink and then he asked, "What did Gaspard do to you?"

Kate didn't answer.

"Your husband will not need to know but I need to know because we have him and we are going to punish him for what he did. But I need you to tell me what he did."

"He ripped my dress and he burned and cut me. He told me that I lied and all I did was tell the truth." A tear slid down her cheek and she mopped it up with part of her dress.

"What did you tell them?" coaxed Iolo.

Kate realised what danger she was in and refused to answer. Reading her face, Iolo said, "Don't worry, I know you told Jorge which way Caradoc was going. But I think Gaspard did something to you after you spoke to Jorge. By the way, Jorge and his men are all dead. They can do you no further harm."

He let his last comment hang in the air. Kate sat very still, taking in what he had just said. The inn seemed to be silent. She was drawn out of herself by the clicking of the dice that Will and Huw were watching.

"They're dead? But there were so many of them and they were so well armed."

"They were looking for one wounded boy and they found thirty fully armed Welshmen looking for someone to punish. Caradoc's father was very angry about how his son was shot and he's very grateful for the help you gave him. The poultice you put on his would probably saved his life. I want you to know that we will bear you no harm. I am only interested in what Gaspard asked you and, if you want to tell me, what he did to you." Iolo let his words sink in. "All I want to know is why Gaspard and his men were hunting Caradoc."

Kate brushed the blonde hair from her eyes. "He wanted to know where Caradoc was going and all I could tell him was that he was on the road to Clun. But the bastard said he didn't believe me. He told me I lied and then he tortured me by cutting me and then he used a hot iron."

She shuddered at the memory of Gaspard putting his hands on her. She remembered how he enjoyed her terror and how he cut her with his dagger. Not large wounds but very small incisions so that the blood just welled up through the skin of her breasts.

"He cut me and then he rubbed salt in the wounds, then when he got bored with that he burned me with a poker and poured cold water on the burns. The cell in the gatehouse is cold and he took away my clothes so that I got very cold. I thought I was going to die."

She shuddered again at the memory and Iolo could see how badly she was affected by her experience. It would haunt her in her dreams.

"I'll make sure he will never do that again to you or anyone else," he said solemnly. "I promise."

She looked into his eyes and saw that he meant it. "Thank you."

"Did he do anything else?" probed Iolo, knowing he was getting into dangerous territory.

"I think you know he did, but I don't want Will to know. He's such a good man and I don't want to hurt him. If he found out he would want to do something and he's not that sort of man. He's strong in his own way, but he could not fight a man like Gaspard."

"Then I suggest you don't speak of this with your husband, and I want you to promise that you won't tell anyone about people on the road again."

Kate nodded her head. She realised that she was being given a last warning.

Iolo relaxed back into his seat and smiled. "Good, would you like another drink to seal our little bargain?"

Kate nodded and Iolo waved to the serving wench to bring more drinks. He waited until the drinks were poured and then asked, "Did Gaspard know the messenger or who the message was for?"

"No, I don't think so because he asked for the boy's name but I didn't have it and he also asked about the message. But the boy didn't have one, at least not when he got to us. He was in such bad shape I didn't think he'd survive the day with that wound in his shoulder."

"Well, he's at home now with his mother, she'll take good care of him. He may come and see you when he's recovered and I don't think you should tell him about what we've just discussed. Just accept his thanks and leave it at that. I wouldn't say anything to his brother or father either; they may not be as understanding as my master and I am."

Kate nodded and took another gulp of her drink.

"Good, I think we understand each other. If you cross me I may just drop a word in Caradoc's brother's ear and he is not a very understanding man. Be warned, you may get a visit from Sir Edmund Mortimer, he's your landlord I believe. I think you should tell him as little as possible without lying." Iolo slid a small purse across the table and pushed it into her hand. "Buy yourself a new dress and I'll let you know if I need anything else."

He stood up and stretched, picked up his tankard and walked over to where Huw was losing at dice. The big man looked up and smiled. "Care for a wager?"

Will sensed something had been said and went over to where his wife was sitting.

"Kate, are you alright?" he asked. "You've gone very pale."

"I'm fine," she said. "I just want to go home and forget that this ever happened."

Montgomery Castle

At first light two parties of men were getting ready to leave the confines of the castle. Lord Rhys was the first to go and he led his men back the way they had come towards the small market town of Newtown in the Severn Valley. They rode through the small walled town and under the base of the ridge on which the castle stood. Sir Edmund's men let them out of Arthur's gate and they rode north-west into the Severn Valley.

Lord de Grey's men were preparing for their journey when Sir Edmund called Lord de Grey and took him for a walk round the battlements where the wind whipped in from the west and the sound of their voices was carried away into the cold grey sky of the morning. They looked out over the broad valley of the river Severn. The fertile land stretched lush and green before them towards Welshpool to the north-east.

Sir Edmund explained, "Lord Rhys is a very good man. He campaigned with the John of Gaunt in France and Castile. I have persuaded him that peace is the best way forward but many of his countrymen are not happy with English rule and they don't like King Henry because of how he treated his tenants on the Bohun estates in Brecon." He paused to catch his breath in the fierce wind. "Rhys is useful and if we're to keep our power here we need to play Henry off against the threat of a Welsh rebellion."

Lord de Grey considered what Sir Edmund had said. "There's land for the taking and I am going to take it. These Welsh peasants can't hold out against our armies. We have to control them or they will cause our English serfs to want the same privileges. I think you're exaggerating the problem. When have the Welsh ever united to fight as one? They're always fighting and feuding amongst themselves."

"Be careful about invading their lands. Rhys told you exactly what they'll do; they've done it before and I have no doubt they'll do it again. Why do you think Edward the First built such a strong ring of castles in Wales? Do you know how much of his treasury he poured into stone?"

"I know what my castles cost to keep up and they are not cheap. And I don't need any lectures from you about lands in Wales; you hold the whole of swathes Montgomeryshire and Radnorshire and almost as many castles as the king in Wales."

"I hold them because I work with my people but the Welsh don't see things the way we do. We have imposed our laws and ways on them. They have their own laws, traditions and a very old history and language. Let's face it, most Welshmen don't speak English and many of our aristocracy speak French as a first language. So if we can't talk to them no wonder they don't understand us." Sir Edmund could see he was not winning his argument with Lord Grey. "The boy who was shot is one of the more educated ones; he speaks Welsh and English and has some French and Latin. We need men like him to deal with the rest, don't you see that?"

"I'll think on what you've said." Lord Grey started back towards the stairs down from the battlements. He turned and said, "Then I suppose the best way forward would be to make them all speak English or French."

"Can you do that? And can you do that with the Scots and Irish as well? Even the Breton's have their own language; have the French wiped that out?"

"Probably not. I have a question for you, why do you call him Lord Rhys?" asked Lord Grey with genuine interest. "After all, the edict from parliament in the year of our Lord 1284 says that no Welshman can hold land and he can't be higher than an esquire in the army."

"Because he is a Welsh lord by ancestry and he can trace his ancestors back for hundreds of years. If I treat him with respect I can act as his overlord and he accepts it, if only in name. Generally he does my bidding and we are both better off because of it."

"I'll think on what you have said but I will conquer my part of Wales and take it by force if necessary."

"Think on what Rhys said before you do anything rash, Wales can be a harsh country," advised Sir Edmund as he pulled his cloak around him.

"A discussion for another time. I have to be on my way." Lord Grey replied as he had grown tired of Sir Edmund's warnings.

Lord Grey turned to face the younger man as an afterthought. "I want Gaspard back; sent me news when you have him."

"I wouldn't raise my hopes too high on that score. If they've got him and he admits to shooting the boy then he's dead. He may already be dead but if he isn't then I pray he'll be returned to us."

Lord de Grey sneered, "If I don't get him back I'll make the buggers pay with their lives."

"Make sure it's not with *your* life. There was a lot of truth in what Lord Rhys told you," Mortimer reiterated, knowing his words had fallen on deaf ears.

Lord de Grey snorted and walked away. Sir Edmund watched the lord as he disappeared into the tower. He slowly followed him down the stairs and into the bailey where the men were waiting. Lord de Grey was issuing orders to his sergeant to collect the remains of his force in Shrewsbury and to take them to Oswestry where he would meet them.

Sir Edmund watched from the battlements as Eric, the sergeant, left with two men for Shrewsbury. Lord Grey led the rest of his men down through the small town and could be seen riding north-east across the Severn Valley towards the border town of Welshpool.

Clanmerwig

Lord Rhys led his men through the hamlet of Llanmerwig and up the valley made by the river Mule. They arrived at Ednyfed's farm as the sun was due south at noon. Mags came out of the house into the yard which was crowded with armed men. She soon spotted Lord Rhys and walked over to him. He dismounted and passed the reins of his horse to his squire.

Lord Rhys announced himself. "Good day, Mags, where's Ednyfed? I need to speak with him."

Mags looked round at Lord Rhys and all his men. "Just to speak with him?"

"Yes, I've just had to escort Lord de Grey of Ruthin to see Sir Edmund Mortimer and I now have to speak with Ednyfed," said Rhys insistently.

She looked up at the sun shielding her eyes with her hand and said, "He'll be back soon for something to eat. Why don't you tell your men to water their horses and I'll get some food on. If I'd known you were coming I could have had some food ready."

"Thank you. I'll let some of the men go home but a bite to eat would be most welcome."

Mags turned and went into her kitchen to prepare the food and speak to Caradoc.

Lord Rhys turned and waved his hand in the air. "Water your horses and eat. Ieuan, dismiss the men who have the furthest to ride home but keep about ten men, a mixture of bowmen and men-at-arms."

Lord Rhys removed his gloves and went to the kitchen. He entered and Mags looked up. "There will only be fourteen men staying to eat."

"I have bread, ham and cheese. I'll cut it up and bring it out on some trenchers."

Rhys nodded and returned outside to wait with his men. What he did not see was Caradoc slipping out of the window on the far side of the house. The boy was soon under the cover of a hedge and working his way down the hill to the old fort where his father was with his brother Owain. As soon as he was out of hearing range he started to run. He was still very weak but his mother insisted that he find his father and tell him of Lord Rhys's arrival.

It took him half an hour to reach the old fort. He scrambled over the grass-covered rampart and he found his father and brother and a few other men in the middle of the fort. Iolo and Huw had also just arrived from Shrewsbury and were dismounting from their horses.

Caradoc walked over to his father and said in Welsh, "Mam sent me to find you. Lord Rhys is at the farm wanting to talk to you."

"Before you go, you should hear what I learned from the farmer's wife," Iolo said, using the same language as he stepping in front of Ednyfed.

"What did she tell you that's so important?"

"She told me Gaspard, the sergeant, tortured her and then raped her. I promised her that he'll not live beyond this day," said Iolo emphatically.

"What is her husband going to do about it?" asked Ednyfed.

"He doesn't know about the rape and while we have her secret, we'll have an informant on the other side of the border. She is scared of him finding out. If she doesn't comply with what we want, we tell her husband."

"Iolo, you tread on dangerous ground. Will was good to Caradoc and I won't have him abused. The secret stays with us, but I agree with you Gaspard dies. Before we kill him let's see what his lordship wants?"

Ednyfed and Iolo mounted their horses and Ednyfed pulled Caradoc up onto his horse behind him.

As they were about to leave Ednyfed said to Owain, "Keep a man on lookout for a signal arrow. If you see one take Gaspard and gag him and keep him out of sight because Lord Rhys has been obdurate in his demands. If we don't return by nightfall, kill him. If we bring Rhys here I'll bring him the long way round and send Mags to warn you."

Owain nodded his understanding and sent two men to the south-western side of the fort to keep watch.

Ednyfed and Iolo rode south so that they could enter the farmyard from the road between Ceri and Newtown so that Lord Rhys would not know where they we holding their English prisoners.

By the time they reached the farm most of Lord Rhys's men had departed for their homes. The ten men that were still waiting on the lord were lying on the sheaves of hay in the barn. Iolo slid from the saddle and took his horse to get some water as he had travelled non-stop from Shrewsbury. Once he had the horse settled he rejoined Ednyfed, whose horse was being led away to the barn by Caradoc.

Lord Rhys came from talking to Ieuan. "Good to see you, Ednyfed. I hear you retrieved Caradoc's pack?"

"We did. We did indeed," said Ednyfed, shuffling his feet uncomfortably. He did not like being under his lordship's scrutiny. It dawned on him that Lord Rhys had planted a spy in his troop who had made the journey over the border.

"I had to stop Lord de Grey at Abermule because someone set fire to an inn in Shrewsbury." Lord Rhys left his comment hanging between them as Iolo's face broke into a sinister smile.

"Why didn't you do us all a favour and kill the bastard then?" Iolo asked pointedly.

"Because I was warned of his presence by Sir Edmund Mortimer, and he would not have been happy with a dead marcher lord on his territory. He has enough on his plate with his nephew, the Earl of March, a hostage in the king's household."

"Why should we care if one Englishman kills another? I would have thought it an ideal opportunity," said Iolo as he kicked the ground.

"You would and then we'd have a royal army here instead of in Scotland. We don't have the manpower to defeat the English," snapped the lord, who was getting tired of Iolo's comments and attitude.

Ednyfed listened to the exchange without comment. He now knew why Lord Rhys was here and what he wanted. He watched Lord Rhys's eyes and waited for the man to ask.

"Your wife has kindly provided my men with meat and drink; will you thank her for me?" asked Rhys, trying to draw Ednyfed into the conversation.

Ednyfed nodded his ascent but still did not speak. Iolo continued, "The more English we kill, even in ones and twos, the better. All we have to do is hit them and run to the hills and they'll never catch us. I think *you* are too fond of the Mortimers, you forget Roger tried to take the throne a few years back and it's said that the boy, the young Earl of March, has a better claim to the throne than the present king. Henry is uncomfortable on his throne."

"You speak treason and you could get us all killed." Lord Rhys turned to Ednyfed. "I must speak with you in private."

"There's nothing you can say to me that Iolo and Caradoc cannot hear. Iolo has ridden with me and I trust his judgement."

Lord Rhys didn't like it but heard something behind him. He looked round and found Caradoc standing just a few feet away from him. He wanted to ask for the English prisoners away from the men and especially away from Iolo.

Caradoc moved to his father's side and looked squarely at Lord Rhys. "You want to let the bastard who shot me go free, don't you?" Caradoc accused.

"You don't understand the politics at work here, boy. It's much more complicated than you can understand."

"Then explain it to me," demanded the young man. He pointed to his shoulder which was still bound with bandages. "You want us to let the man who shot me go free? Who will punish him for what he did? Or isn't it a crime to shoot a Welshman now?"

Lord Rhys's face turned red with embarrassment as he had not expected to be assailed by young Caradoc. He took a deep breath to regain his composure. "Of course it's not right that you should have been shot but there are other things to take into consideration here. The next time Lord de Grey comes he will be prepared and I'll not be able to stop him."

Iolo chimed in, "Who asked you to? If he'd have got anywhere near us we'd have killed him. After all, he can't have that many men left."

"What do you mean by that?" Rhys demanded.

"Well, he's already lost a patrol of nine or so men plus those he lost in the fire in Shrewsbury, not counting the two we found when we were looking for Caradoc's pack," said Ednyfed. He watched Rhys's face and could see the horror on his face as he realised just how much damage these men had inflicted upon the marcher lord. Ednyfed could see the impact of his words written on the man's features.

Ednyfed asked, "Why exactly have you come here?"

Lord Rhys drew himself up to his full height and demanded, "You will turn any English prisoners you have over to me, NOW. I will return them to Sir Edmund and that will be the end of the matter."

Ednyfed threw back his head and laughed aloud and looked around at Ieuan and the rest of the men lounging in the barn. "I think you've had a wasted trip."

Lord Rhys realised his authority was gone. Ednyfed nodded and Iolo stepped away from the group, drew an arrow, notched it and loosed it into the sky. The arrow flew high into the sky and then plummeted back to earth. Rhys knew exactly what had happened: the signal for the Englishmen to die had been sent and there was nothing he could do about it. He felt despair as he knew Sir Edmund would be angry and Lord Grey apoplectic and would return as he had promised with a small army.

"You don't know what you've done!" the lord moaned.

"I think I've just taken a measure of justice," said Ednyfed. "Now I'd like the traitor to our nation to leave my farm."

Iolo nocked another arrow and pointed roughly in the direction of Lord Rhys.

Lord Rhys did not like being called a traitor and he started to order Ieuan to get his men ready to arrest Ednyfed when the realised that all his men were bunched together in the farmyard and that Ednyfed probably had men hiding, waiting for his signal. So he responded angrily, "You should remember just who you hold your lands from."

"I know full well who I hold my lands from and if he wants them back he can come and try to take them, personally. And anyone he sends to take the farm will go the same way as Gaspard." Ednyfed paused and then said to Iolo, "I think you should enlighten his lordship about the kind of man Lord Grey employs."

"Gaspard tortured and raped the wife of Will, the farmer who helped Caradoc, to get information about where the boy had gone. This was the wife of one of Sir Edmund Mortimer's tenants. Do you think Mortimer will let that go? But what you're saying is there will be no justice for Caradoc here, who was nearly killed by Lord Grey's men, and there will be no justice for the farmer's wife who was in the wrong place at the wrong time. Do you still want to let this animal go free? After all, next time it could be your wife or daughter."

"If you put that to Sir Edmund I'm sure he'll listen," said Ednyfed sounding mockingly reasonable.

"No! He won't, because the woman will not admit to being raped for fear of losing her husband and Sir Edmund should have demanded Gaspard's arrest for shooting Caradoc. That has not happened and I assume from what you've said so far today that you've spoken with him recently."

"We could still present him with the facts when we hand this Gaspard over to him," said Lord Rhys, almost pleading. He knew his cause was lost, and was trying to think of a way of explaining the situation to Sir Edmund so he would understand his predicament.

"And Sir Edmund will hand him back to his master to be used against us again. No, he's a dead man." Ednyfed made his bald statement and let it sink in before continuing. "I suggest that if you don't want to be involved that you go home."

Lord Rhys was indignant. "Who are you to tell me to go home, this *is* my business."

"Not if you interfere with our Welsh justice. Tell Sir Edmund that you could find no sign of Gaspard." He spread his arms wide and turned in a circle. "Can you find him here? I don't think so!"

Ednyfed paused for a response. "No! Then go home. I thank you for your warning but it is not needed. If Sir Edmund asks, we will ask him to find evidence of Lord Grey's sergeant. After all, he probably died in the fire in Shrewsbury you just told us about."

Lord Rhys lost his patience. "I came here to help you but I can see you are hell bent on destruction. Sir Edmund knows who you are?"

"And who told him?" interrupted Iolo. "You?"

Lord Rhys ignored Iolo and spoke directly to Ednyfed, "You were seen in Clun, and they now know Caradoc is your son."

"As Iolo says, who told him? Sir Edmund has so many lands, it is unlikely he would remember one farmer or one shepherd. This land is ours and always has been. I pay no homage to an English lord for it. If Sir Edmund comes I'll speak to him but if he forces me, I may not be as polite as I'm being with you. I suggest you tell the English to stay on their side of Offa's Dyke – that's why it was built, to keep us out of Mercia and them out of Cymru."

Lord Rhys's frustration was showing on his face. He had already told Sir Edmund that he would speak to Ednyfed and Mortimer was not the most temperate of men. He waved Ieuan to come over.

"Ieuan, take the men to Newtown and keep them there and don't let them get drunk." Lord Rhys commanded.

"My lord? Do you want me to return? Who do you want to stay with you?"

"Just my squire. Now go," Lord Rhys ordered irritably.

Ieuan called the men from the barn and had them form up. Within five minutes they were riding northwards down the hill to the small market town by the river Severn. Lord Rhys waited until his men were out of sight and then he turned to Ednyfed and said, "Let's go and see Gaspard. I want to question him before you kill him. When I've finished with him either you give him to me or you kill him. But I *will* speak to him."

Ednyfed nodded and walked away to the kitchen to speak with his wife.

Iolo, who was still standing near, said, "You're wasting your breath. Gaspard's a murderous bastard and he's a very dangerous animal. But I think you know that. Why do you want to talk to him?"

Rhys sagged in frustration. "For my own peace of mind. I know you won't understand that but I need to see if I think he's guilty of what you accuse him of."

Ednyfed returned with Caradoc to where the two men were waiting.

"If you want to see him I'll take you but you have to be blindfolded and if I think we're being followed it'll be you and your squire that suffer."

"So you're threatening *me* now?" asked Lord Rhys in a tone which was non-threatening. He had to see Gaspard so he could make his own judgement of the man.

"Not through choice. I just want the boy to be secure. I also want your assurance that my sons are not implicated in any way when you report to Sir Edmund . . ." Ednyfed held his hand up to stop Lord Rhys from interrupting, ". . . as I know you will, that the blame will rest with me and me alone. Do I have your word?"

"You do. What has happened is not of our making but we must deal with what has happened as it is," said Lord Rhys, distancing himself from the position of the marcher lords. "Sir Edmund was going to have a word with Lord Grey before he rode north but I doubt if that will change the arrogant bastard's mind. He told me last night if he doesn't get his men back he'll come back with a force of his own men."

"Mortimer won't like that and we'll just move back into the hills. So let him come and find us if he can."

"I told him that but this is 'Lord Reginald de Grey' we are talking about and I doubt he'll listen to reason from anyone; he certainly didn't want to listen to me. He will only back down if directly ordered to do so by the king and I can't see the king doing that."

"You should have let him through and we could have killed him now and saved ourselves the problem in the future," said Iolo, still goading Lord Rhys.

"And then Sir Edmund really would have had to do something about it and he knows this country better than any of his fellow marcher lords. He also has many Welshmen as retainers who are loyal to him."

"Including you?" Iolo jibed.

"I don't know what my decision will be just yet but I have no wish to have another campaign running round these mountains if I can possibly avoid it. I'm beginning to feel my age. As I get older diplomacy becomes more agreeable. Now let's get going."

Ednyfed blindfolded both the older lord and his young squire. They were helped to mount their horses and Ednyfed led the party south from the farmyard. They rode for two hours with Ednyfed laying false trails and doubling back several times to ensure they were not being followed.

Eventually he led Lord Rhys into the old fort from the woods to the south of it. He helped the older man from his horse and removed his blindfold. Rhys rubbed his eyes and looked around and burst out laughing. "I should have guessed."

He recognised that he was only about a mile or so from Ednyfed's farm. He walked round the fort to stretch his legs after the ride. He noted the number of guards and was glad he had sent his men away. He did not want to spill any more Welsh blood if he could possibly avoid it. While he was walking round his squire brought him some water to drink.

Ednyfed and Owain dragged the bedraggled figure of Gaspard from the small lean-to and dropped him on the ground near a fire pit by the western wall. Owain started heating some irons and Iolo came over to help him but Ednyfed sent him away because he didn't want him to continue to bait Lord Rhys when he was talking to Gaspard.

Lord Rhys came over and squatted by the prone man. He looked at the man's unkempt appearance and could see evidence of the fire in Shrewsbury in black smudges on his face and clothes.

"I'm going to ask you some questions," Ednyfed said in his native Welsh, taking charge. "If you answer honestly then it'll go easier with you. Do you understand me?"

Gaspard pulled himself into a sitting position and stared blankly at him. Owain translated what his father had said first into English and then into French.

Rhys said to Ednyfed in Welsh, "I'll question him in English and Owain can translate for you."

Rhys knew Ednyfed could speak English but also knew that he wasn't as fluent as his son appeared to be. He also knew that speaking in Welsh would only slow the interrogation down.

Lord Rhys called Caradoc forward. "Do you recognise this man?" He indicated to Gaspard, who was struggling to sit up.

Caradoc replied in Welsh, "Yes, he was one of the cowards who shot me in the back."

Rhys turned to Gaspard and said in English, "This boy has just identified you as one of the men who shot and nearly killed him. For that alone these men have reason to kill you. Do you understand me?"

Gaspard did not respond. Lord Rhys kicked him and then Gaspard nodded his agreement.

"Why did you shoot the boy?"

"We thought he was the messenger Lord de Grey had sent us out to find," answered the sergeant glumly. He tugged at the ropes binding his hands but the bonds were too tight.

"How did you identify the boy as the messenger? I have talked to his father and he had no messages, just good wishes from his uncle who is a monk in Oxford."

"He was on the ridge and he was travelling very light. He had a bow and a falchion and was scanning the valley from the ridge. It was a foul night and so no one in his right mind would be travelling if he could avoid it. He had no pack and so, as there was no one else abroad that night. So we assumed that he must be the messenger Lord Grey was expecting."

"Why didn't you ask him if he was a messenger?" asked Lord Rhys, trying to be reasonable.

"He's Welsh, he'd have lied," said Gaspard belligerently. He was beginning to feel that this man might get him away from his captors. His despair started to lift.

Lord Rhys looked down on the man at his feet. "You should be very careful what you say, you might offend somebody. We're all Welsh here and I don't think any of the men I see here has ever lied to me."

Lord Rhys continued his questioning. "What did you do with the blonde woman, the farmer's wife?"

Gaspard looked up, startled, but did not answer. *How did this man know about the blonde woman? Why would he care? After all, she was just a peasant.*

"I take it you do remember the farmer's wife you tortured in Ludlow Castle and then kidnapped and took away with you to Shrewsbury? She was found tied up in your room at The Lion inn."

Gaspard nodded warily. He did not like the way the line of questioning was going. It certainly did not seem to be going his way.

"She says you raped her and she also says you cut her and burned her with a heated iron." Iolo had taken great pleasure in telling Lord Rhys every detail he had gleaned from Kate on the ride from the farm. He had embellished Kate's words and so Lord Rhys was not happy about the man he saw before him. Even if half of what Iolo had said he had done was true then the man deserved to die.

Gaspard still said nothing. He despaired – how did this man know about the woman? Who was she anyway? A nobody, just another greedy little informer. Gaspard realised that he should use that against her.

No one had noticed that Iolo had moved closer to the prisoner.

"The reason she was at the castle was she told Lord de Grey's other sergeant Jorge where she had seen the boy." He nodded toward Caradoc. "I was just making sure she hadn't just made up a story to claim a reward."

"So you tortured her but did you have to rape her?" snapped Iolo in disgust.

"Who says I did? The slattern?" said Gaspard, trying to sound indignant.

"I think at this point I would rather believe her than believe you. After all you are a man who attempted to murder a young man for no reason other than he was the only person travelling that night. You didn't even give him a chance to deny he was the man you were looking for."

Iolo had heard Gaspard's raised voice and had crept closer to the prisoner behind Lord Rhys's back. Ednyfed was so intend on listening to Gaspard that he had not noticed Iolo's approach.

Gaspard took the initiative. "What I did was in the service of Lord de Grey. I do not answer to you. When the lord finds me he'll have all your heads on a pike."

Iolo lost his temper and lashed out with his foot, smashing Gaspard's nose. Blood flowed down his face as he fell onto his back. Ednyfed pushed Iolo away from the prone sergeant.

Rhys looked down at Gaspard. "Do you inspire this much enmity in all men?" He didn't wait for an answer but turned to Ednyfed and said in Welsh, "If you can't keep him under control, send him home. If he wants to stay tell him to stand over there." He indicated to a spot a dozen feet away.

Iolo saw the look of disgust Ednyfed was giving him and walked to the spot Lord Rhys had indicated. Lord Rhys turned back to the prisoner.

"So, we have attempted murder of the boy and the torture and rape of the farmer's wife. What do you think Sir Edmund Mortimer will do when I present you to him with witnesses to what you have done?"

"Sir Edmund will give me back to Lord de Grey if he knows what's good for him," said Gaspard defiantly.

"That's what I think will happen and you are clearly unrepentant for what you have done so I'm leaving you in Ednyfed's hands. You are scum. You give honest soldiers a bad name. I think the world will be a better place without you."

Lord Rhys turned to Ednyfed and, changing to Welsh, said, "I can find nothing redeeming in this man and I agree with him, if we give him to Sir Edmund he'll just hand him over to Lord de Grey. Can you make him disappear with no trace to be found, *ever?*"

"I can and I will," replied Ednyfed. "What will you say to Sir Edmund?"

"I asked you about your travels over the border and whether you encountered Gaspard. You said you hadn't seen him. I'll say I've spoken to Caradoc and I'll give Sir Edmund the description Caradoc has given me of the men who shot him. The main description being of that piece of shit." He turned and kicked Gaspard in the side. "I'll also tell him about the fire at the inn in Shrewsbury and say that the sergeant could have been one of those who went up in smoke. Then I'll let him draw his own conclusions."

Lord Rhys looked around the fort and said, "I'm getting tired of all this. Can you have my squire bring my horse, I think I'll rest in Newtown this evening."

Caradoc went to get the squire while Iolo and Owain dragged Gaspard away. As soon as they had him back by the lean-to Owain drew a dagger from his boot and stabbed Gaspard in the liver and then in the kidney, then with a practised move he pulled the sergeant's head back and sliced through his windpipe and the jugular vein in his throat in one fluid movement. The blood spurted out onto the ground and the sergeant let out his last breath with a whimper, and Owain dropped the corpse to the ground by the wall.

Owain's swift action took Iolo completely by surprise. Iolo looked at Owain. "Why did you do that?"

"My father wanted him dead and he is," said the younger man in a tone that was not to be argued with. Owain walked back to where Ednyfed was helping Lord Rhys up onto his horse. The lord adjusted himself in the saddle and made ready to ride.

"It's done, he's dead," said Owain, and Ednyfed acknowledged him with a nod.

"Why don't you ride with me, young man? I think we have things to discuss," invited Lord Rhys as he turned his horse towards the fort's gate.

Ednyfed met Owain's eyes. There was agreement in them so the younger man went to get his horse. Iolo had caught up with Owain as the lord was speaking to him. He was about to say something when Ednyfed grabbed his arm and turned him away. Lord Rhys left with his squire and Owain following him through the opening that acted as a gate for the old fort.

Iolo was mad; he had wanted to kill Gaspard slowly, causing him the maximum pain.

Ednyfed turned on him. "He's dead?"

"Yes," he said, nodding his head.

"Then let's get rid of the body and end it."

"I wanted to cause him some of the pain he caused Kate, Will's wife. Did you not want to punish him for what he did to Caradoc?"

"And what good would that have done? I told Owain to kill him quickly and have it done with. We'll feed his body to the pigs but he'll have to be cut up first."

"That's a messy job," protested Iolo.

"And you're going to help me do it." He walked off and set men to return the fort to as it had been when they arrived. Two men went to bring some pigs down from the farm and Caradoc returned to the farm with them.

When everyone else had been set their tasks Ednyfed said to Iolo, "If you must kill someone, go and kill the other bowman who shot Owain. We'll cut up both bodies and feed them to the pigs. I'll drain Gaspard's blood while you kill the bowman. We need to burn all their clothes and any money from their pouches can be given to the poor."

Iolo found William bound hand and foot in a small tent near the wall on the opposite side of the fort to where Gaspard had been held. Iolo pulled William out of the shelter and sat him with his back to the wall.

"You're a dead man," said Iolo. "You can die quickly and painlessly or you can die slowly, I don't mind."

William nodded his head and strained against his bonds.

"I ask the questions and you answer. If the answers are good and I can tell by your face you're telling the truth, then you die quickly. Tell lies and you will feel a great deal of pain."

Iolo studied the man's face before he continued. "Lord Grey isn't coming. Lord Rhys took him back to Sir Edmund Mortimer at Montgomery Castle. So no help is coming and out here you can scream as much as you like."

Iolo removed the gag from William's mouth and gave him some water to drink from a flask. William shifted himself into a more comfortable position.

"What do you want to know?" William was resigned to his fate but he wanted it to end quickly. He could do without the pain and he wasn't into heroics when there was no one around to see them.

"Why did you shoot the boy?" Iolo asked already knowing the answer that Gaspard had given.

"Gaspard thought he was the messenger Lord de Grey was waiting for. There was no one else on the road so we assumed that the boy was the one."

"Why didn't you question him first before shooting him?" Iolo asked, hearing Ednyfed come up behind him.

"Gaspard assumed that he was the messenger, so why take the risk? Gaspard couldn't see a pack and the man was armed with a bow and a falchion. I did say to Gaspard that I thought a messenger would be mounted but he wouldn't listen."

Iolo watched William's eyes; they were relaxed and he seemed to be telling the truth. "Do you know what the message was about?"

"No, just that it was important to Lord de Grey. Gaspard was very good at keeping things like that to himself. He liked being the only one who knew what his lordship was up to. Lord Grey can be very devious when it's in his interests. But I'm just a soldier following orders and I'm too old to find a new lord."

"Tell me about Lord de Grey?"

"What's to know? He's a typical arrogant bastard. His family came over with the conqueror and he holds lands in the south-east of England and in Cheshire and north Wales and I think he wants more. His type are never satisfied with what they've got, they always want more. The king owes him for his support in taking the throne so I think he's planning to take advantage of his new-found favour. He'll keep pushing until someone stops him."

Iolo realised he was not going to get the answer he had been expecting so he stepped forward and drove the poniard he had concealed behind his back through William's right eye. The old archer didn't know what hit him; he was dead before he knew it. Blood poured onto the ground and soaked the earth.

Iolo looked over at Ednyfed. "He didn't know much, so I suppose we're better rid of them both."

Ednyfed nodded and they picked up the dead archer and carried him over to the trench Ednyfed had had dug earlier. They stripped him and laid him next to Gaspard's corpse.

They worked into the night, eventually working by torch light. By morning all that could be found in the old fort was a pen of ten pigs feeding from a trough. The lean to had gone and there was a fire burning in a pit at the centre of the fort. Iolo and Ednyfed were washing the blood from their bodies as the sun came up. The rest of the men had long since gone to their homes.

"They'll never find them now," said Iolo as he watched the pigs eating the dismembered corpses.

"Find who?" asked Ednyfed with a mischievous smile.

"As you say," Iolo said as he caught Ednyfed's mood. "Can I ask you a question?"

Ednyfed nodded.

"Why did you send Owain with Lord Rhys?"

"To make sure his lordship wouldn't return while we were at work. I also know that Lord Rhys now thinks of me as someone he can't control." He paused. "Maybe even as an enemy. He has no such feelings about Owain, yet. He will try to make Owain spy on me. And I will have Owain tell him what I want him to hear, but Owain will give him enough good information so that the misinformation is disguised."

Ednyfed looked into Iolo's eyes and said, "I think you should go on a long trip. You've offended the old man and he has a habit of taking his revenge. He doesn't take people challenging his authority very well. I suggest you take a ride south to Brecon. You may find employment down there for a while. We'll meet again, I'm sure."

Ednyfed turned away and picked up his shirt. As he put it on he asked Iolo, "What do you think about this messenger Gaspard was talking about?"

Iolo answered, "I think that any messenger would have been riding a horse. If possible, he would have crossed the border with a party of other riders if he could and he wouldn't have drawn attention to himself if he could possibly have avoided it."

"Then you'd better go and deliver it, hadn't you," said Ednyfed as he walked away leaving Iolo standing in the middle of the little fort.

Vale of Ceri – Newtown

A rider watched the two men from the shadows of the woods to the south, which overlooked the old hill fort. He waited for a full hour after all the men had departed before he rode down to inspect their handiwork. He dismounted, hobbled his horse and left it to graze outside the small fort. He did not want his horse's tracks visible inside the fort for Ednyfed to know that he was being spied upon.

The man moved round the fort, checking the site of the lean-to and the pen where the pigs were being held. He found the fire pit but only because he had seen the fire from his vantage point. The cut in the turf was hardly visible and it would disappear with a few days of bad weather as the wind and rain would smear the line cut into the ground into nothing.

The spy walked round the outside of the fort, looking for any signs of the fort's occupation, but was soon satisfied that Ednyfed's men had been diligent in removing the signs of the past days. Even the tracks of the horses had been disguised by having the pigs run over them.

When he was satisfied nothing remained of Lord de Grey's men he returned his horse, making sure he left no tracks, and rode north-west to report to his master. He rode slowly leaving few tracks. Every few minutes he stopped and watched his back-trail to make sure he was not being followed; he did not want his presence known to anyone as it could jeopardise his living.

When he arrived at Newtown he stabled his horse, making sure he had a good feed of oats. The spy went to find Lord Rhys at The Checkers inn on the town's Broad Street. He entered, unseen, by the backdoor and went straight up to Lord Rhys's room. Rory, the spy, knocked on the door and entered without waiting for a response. Lord Rhys waved him in and Tegwyn stood up and asked, "Well, what happened?"

"When I inspected the old fort there was no trace of the bodies. Ednyfed and his men did a good job in cleaning up. There is no trace that anyone was there except the pigs. Anyone searching would have to know exactly what they were looking for and where. A few days of the pigs churning around and there will be nothing to see at all except a mud patch. I shouldn't worry about those men being found."

"Do we know any more about this mysterious messenger Lord de Grey's men were trying to find?" asked Tegwyn. "Do you think Ednyfed knows more than he's saying?"

"No, I think Ednyfed was involved because of his son and most of the men on the raid were locals. There were only one or two I didn't recognise." Rhys paused as he thought about the men he had seen with Ednyfed.

"What about Iolo? He and Ednyfed had a long talk while they were working on disposing of the bodies," answered Rory.

Lord Rhys added, "I don't know him at all. He was the one who was most vociferous in wanting to kill the Englishmen and he seemed to know most about what Gaspard had done with the farmer's wife. What do we know about him?"

"Not much," said Tegwyn. "The first time I saw him was at Ednyfed's farm when they were getting ready to go on their raid across the border."

"Rory find Gwyn Mochyn and have him find this Iolo and follow him. If he is the messenger then at least we'll know who the message was for."

"Is he the best choice to follow Iolo?" asked Tegwyn, knowing Gwyn Mochyn's reputation as a slippery customer. He did not trust the man, who was known for stealing pigs.

"He's the most dispensable and he won't be traced to us if anything goes wrong. He's not known as one of my retainers so I can deny him if he's caught," Lord Rhys said.

"What do you think could go wrong?" asked Rory, his curiosity peeked.

"I just don't want Lord de Grey to suspect us of anything, he's too close to the king to be crossed," said Lord Rhys. "If Gwyn gets caught there he won't be traceable back to me. There could be serious consequences and if this message is about what I think it's about then the repercussions could be grave for all of us. So just make sure Gwyn doesn't think you work for me, understand?"

Rory nodded.

"I'll find Gwyn Mochyn and send him to find Iolo. I'll tell him to make sure he doesn't get seen," said Rory as he headed for the door.

"Wait. When you find him, let him think you're working for the Mortimers. I don't think he knows you so that would be feasible. Tell him to report who receives the message to you here are soon as he finds out who it is." Lord Rhys continued, "I don't want any connection with the person who receives the message until I know what is going on. There's something not right about this, so we need to protect ourselves against both the English and whoever has raised Lord Grey's ire."

Rory nodded his head in ascent and left the lord pondering on whom the message was for and its contents. Tegwyn sat silently, thinking about what Rhys had said.

"Why don't you ask Ednyfed where he knows Iolo from?" he asked.

"Because I don't want Ednyfed connecting us with this message," said Lord Rhys, who was starting to think about preparing for the winter. "Go and get some sleep, we have work to do tomorrow."

Newtown – Dolforwyn

Rory found Gwyn Mochyn at the stables about to mount his horse to leave town. It had taken Rory over an hour to find Gwyn and then he had followed him until he was on his own. Rory did not want to be seen talking to Gwyn by any of the townsfolk.

"A word with you, are you Gwyn Mochyn?" asked Rory, knowing exactly who he was. He approached the Welshman cautiously but showing that he was not a threat by keeping his hands clear of his weapons.

"Depends on who's asking," came the curt reply. Gwyn Mochyn looked at the man's hard worn travelling clothes and assumed that he was not a local man. His Welsh was accented with French but the sword at his side meant business.

"I don't want to talk here. I'll get my horse and we can talk on the road. I'm heading for the castle at Dolforwyn," said Rory, knowing that the castle, which was built by Llewellyn ap Gruffydd (the Last), was now in the possession of the Mortimers, thus implying he was one of Sir Edmund's men.

Gwyn considered the man's proposal for a moment. "I suppose I could ride that way to get where I'm going."

Rory quickly saddled his horse and was ready to ride within a few minutes. They left Newtown following a track eastwards to the deserted old motte and bailey castle situated beside the river Severn about a mile east of the town.

Once they were clear of the town, Gwyn asked, "What do you want of me?"

"I need someone to find a man called Iolo and to follow him," said Rory, seeing the interest in Gwyn's eyes.

"And what would that be worth to you?" asked Gwyn, calculating what the job might be worth to the stranger.

Rory pulled some coins from his belt and passed them over. "The same when you come and tell me who he meets and who he talks to over the next three days."

Gwyn Mochyn smelt money but he also smelt trouble. He did not know Iolo well but he had seen him with Ednyfed and could tell that he was not a man to be crossed. He looked at the coins in his hand.

"Just to find him will be worth more than this, following him will be harder. He went over the border with Ednyfed and that means he must be a good man in a fight, or Ednyfed wouldn't have taken him. Find someone else."

Rory took a purse from his pouch and poured out some more coins into Gwyn's outstretched hand.

Gwyn looked Rory directly in the eye. "God, you must be desperate."

"Do we have a deal?"

"Where will you be when I find out who he meets?"

"I'll be in either Newtown, Montgomery or at Dolforwyn Castle. Try Newtown first, I'm looking to set up a business there," said Rory, knowing that the town was growing as a trading centre for wool.

Gwyn Mochyn asked, "Where was Iolo last seen?"

"At Ednyfed's farm over towards the Vale of Ceri."

"Why don't you find him and follow him yourself?" Gwyn asked.

"My accent would give me away and I don't want to raise people's suspicions of me just as I'm starting in business in the town. I need to build trust so people will do business with me."

"What trade are you setting up?" asked Gwyn as he turned his horse to head south.

"I'm a mercer and I trade in wool and cloth," lied Rory smoothly.

"With a little spying on the side," smiled Gwyn as he tucked the money away in his belt pouch. *Mercenary more like,* thought Gwyn Mochyn, who had seen many spies the marcher lords had tried to infiltrate over the border since the 1284 edict.

"How do you think I got permission to trade here? The town is new and I can make a good living here," said Rory convincingly. "This could be the beginning of a profitable relationship for both of us."

Something niggled at Gwyn. He asked, "What made you come and find me?"

"I asked the landlord of The Checkers if there was a man who knew the country who could help with my business of buying wool for the lowest prices," Rory replied as they rode slowly along the river valley with its undulating hills but with high mountains on either side.

Gwyn Mochyn still did not trust the man but he filed the information away with the intention of talking to Hari, the landlord of The Checkers, when he was next in Newtown. He had known Hari a long time. If Rory had spoken to him Hari would give him the whole conversation; the man had an incredibly good memory.

"I'll see you when I find out who Iolo has met with," said Gwyn Mochyn as he turned his horse and rode south towards Ednyfed's farm. He stopped his horse, turned in the saddle and asked, "Oh! Who should I ask for when I'm trying to find you?"

"Rory the mercer, ask for me at The Checkers. I'll let Hari know when I'll be back in Newtown. I shouldn't be hard to find."

Gwyn nodded and started his horse southward. Rory watched the man ride away and then continued on his way towards Dolforwyn Castle, the small Welsh-built fortress just north of where the river Mule flows into the Severn.

Rory forded the river and rode up to what remained of the small village which had once been a town before Roger de Montgomery established his market town at Newtown. He hid his horse in the woods to the west of the village and made his way to the gatehouse on foot as he didn't want to be seen. The castle was smaller than the castle at Montgomery but it was still a good climb to get to it. The castle appeared suddenly above the skyline, dark and sombre.

At the gatehouse Rory was admitted and led across the inner courtyard to the hall.

Sir Edmund Mortimer was working at a table in the hall as Rory was admitted. He looked up. "I wasn't expecting you today. What's happened?"

"The sergeant, Gaspard, and the archer are dead and you won't find the bodies, they've been eaten by hogs. I can also tell you that Jorge and his men were ambushed somewhere near Clun and wiped out," said Rory bluntly, not wanting to waste time as he needed to get back to Lord Rhys.

"Ten men all dead, de Grey won't be pleased with that piece of news. What part did Lord Rhys have in this?"

"He had nothing to do with the ambush because he was in Newtown with Tegwyn and me. But he did talk to Ednyfed before the other two were killed. I think Lord Rhys tried to save their lives but the farmer killed them for trying to kill his boy."

Sir Edmund nodded as he took in the information.

"We also think we know who the messenger is and I've just sent a man called Gwyn Mochyn to find him."

"Who is the messenger?" asked Sir Edmund, his attention now fully focused on the spy.

"We think it's a man named Iolo," answered Rory.

"Can we catch him? That might placate de Grey for the loss of his men," said Sir Edmund, thinking aloud.

"We aren't trying to catch him. We want to know who the message was intended for." Rory paused for a breath. "That's why we've sent Gwyn Mochyn to find him and follow him to find out who we will have to deal with. Lord Rhys thinks there's more to this than meets the eye."

Sir Edmund stood up and paced up and down the hall. *It would be good to know who the recipient of the message was,* he thought. He nodded and said, "Let me know what you find out. Now you'd better get back to Rhys before you are missed."

He picked up several coins from the table and passed them to the spy.

"Thank you, my lord," said Rory as he made the coins disappear into his belt pouch.

Rory pulled up his cowl and left the hall. He retraced his steps back to the gatehouse and slipped out of the castle and back to the woods where he had hidden his horse. He walked his horse down the steep track back to the flat of the river valley before mounting.

Rory rode slowly back to Newtown along the north side of the river to report to Lord Rhys. He smiled to himself; having two masters was proving very profitable. He just had to keep them both apart.

As he reached the small church at Llanllwchaiarn the heavens opened and rain fell from the sky. Rory was soaked before he could get into of the shelter of the church.

Vale of Ceri

Gwyn Mochyn arrived at Ednyfed's farm just before noon. He rode into the yard, dismounted and tied his horse to the railed gate leading to the paddock. He looked round the well-ordered farmyard for any sign of the activities of the last few days. There was nothing to show anything was amiss.

Ednyfed came out of the barn to see who had arrived. When he saw who it was he asked gruffly, "What do you want?"

"Just wondered how the boy was doing? It was a nasty wound he had in his shoulder," replied Gwyn, ignoring Ednyfed's hostility.

Ednyfed watched Gwyn with caution but answered, "He's recovering fine. He's up and about now but his shoulder is still causing him some pain. It'll be a while before he's back to his full strength."

"Did you find out who did it? Over the border, I mean," asked Gwyn, trying to get Ednyfed to open up. Ednyfed looked directly into Gwyn's eyes as if he was trying to judge the man.

"I know it wasn't you, if that's what you mean. I'm sorry about my reaction when you brought him home," said Ednyfed, grudgingly knowing that he owed Gwyn for carrying Caradoc home when he could have left him on the road where he found him. If he'd done that the boy would probably be dead instead of getting better with his mother to look after him.

"That's understandable," said Gwyn, being at his most reasonable. "Did everyone get back safely? Only I've heard rumours in Newtown about an English lord rampaging round the border round Clun. I was wondering if it's safe to cross the border or should I leave it for a few days?"

"I'd leave it for a while if you can. I think we stirred up more than we expected to but everyone got back safe. It's not like you to worry about others."

"What a reputation I must have for you to think so ill of me. What did I ever do to you to deserve such . . . I'm glad your boy is on the mend and thank you for the advice. I'll leave my trip for a few days. Maybe I'll go north for a while instead."

"I thought you avoided Oswestry these days," said Ednyfed with a grin.

"So Caradoc told you my little story, did he? Well, I haven't been there for years and I doubt I'll be welcome if I did go there, but they do raise a sweet tasting suckling pig," he laughed.

Ednyfed laughed as well. "Come in and have a drink and see how Caradoc's doing."

Gwyn realised he had managed to break the ice and now he could get a conversation going about the raid across the border. Eventually he would bring the conversation round to Iolo but that could wait until he had seen Caradoc.

The two men walked over to the house and they entered the kitchen where Mags was preparing the evening meal. Ednyfed poured some cider he had rescued from across the border.

Gwyn took a sip and said, "Fine things these Normans do with apples. Amber nectar."

"Caradoc, someone to see you," called Ednyfed as he poured himself a beaker of cider. There was a clatter and Caradoc appeared from one of the bedrooms.

"You're the man who carried me over the Vastre," said Caradoc, recognising Gwyn.

"Well it appears that the burden was worth it. It's good to see you up and about. How's the shoulder healing?" asked Gwyn with genuine interest.

"It getting better but it still aches, especially when it's cold or when I lie on it awkwardly."

"He's lucky to be alive," said his mother, "and he'll have to wait until he's better before he can go off to Strata Florida."

Gwyn was aghast, "What! You're going to become a monk? That's no job for a Welshman."

"Watch what you say, my brother's a monk in Oxford. Caradoc was on his way home from visiting him when he was attacked," snapped Mags angrily.

"No offence meant, just a waste of a good man to the church." He turned to Ednyfed. "What did you learn over the border? Everyone in Newtown is talking about your raid. Did you find out why they tried to kill Caradoc here?"

"Lord de Grey's men thought he was a messenger and they weren't too fussy about who they shot to find him, but keep that to yourself."

"So they didn't find the messenger then, are they still looking?" probed Gwyn.

Ednyfed smiled, "No, Lord de Grey was persuaded to go home to Ruthin, but I suspect he's still looking for that messenger, if he exists. The number of men he had out searching for Caradoc, he must be worried about something."

"Who persuaded him to leave?" asked Gwyn, probing for more information.

"Lord Rhys took him to visit Sir Edmund Mortimer at Montgomery. He wasn't very pleased about it but after that he was seen riding for Welshpool, but I suspect it's not the last we will hear from him," said Ednyfed. "Lord Rhys is worried about what de Grey will do next. Rhys has thrown in his lot with the Mortimers but he's not sure that even they can protect him and his lands against land hungry men like de Grey. The man has the king's ear and the Mortimers are out of favour at the moment."

Gwyn tried a new tack, "I'll keep an eye out for him when I travel north. Who is Lord de Grey afraid of? He seems to be very worried about this message, so who is he afraid of offending?"

"That's a very good question. If we knew that we could join whoever it is in driving the likes of de Grey out of Wales once and for all," said Ednyfed, who was thinking it would be good to know who Iolo was delivering his message to.

"Do you know Iolo who came with us to Clun?" he asked Gwyn.

"Is he the one who was with Huw the other day when you went on your raid?"

"You were watching?" asked Ednyfed surprised that he had been followed.

"I thought I tag along and see what I could pick up but I lost you at Clun," lied Gwyn easily. "So I just came home."

"You didn't miss much, a tiring ride to collect Caradoc's pack but yes, that was Iolo. He was here yesterday and he was talking about going north. If you meet him give him my regards. When he left he was going up the Severn towards Caersws; I think he has relatives there."

Gwyn now knew where his man was going but he had to stay for a while so that he did not arouse suspicion with Ednyfed. He took his time in finishing his cider. He told Caradoc to look after himself and walked out to his horse with the young man.

"You didn't have a horse the day you found me," said Caradoc as Gwyn climbed into his saddle.

"I had him stabled in Newtown but I often walk to places. It's easier sometimes to travel on foot rather than by horse because you don't get noticed. A horse can be hard to hide, especially out on the moors. A man can lie down in a shallow grove in the land but a horse can be seen way off," explained Gwyn. "I'll show you what I mean sometime, when your better and your shoulder has mended."

Gwyn mounted his horse and trotted away. He waved to the boy and his father as he rode back down the steep hill towards Newtown.

———————————

Ednyfed patted Caradoc on his shoulder and said, "I wouldn't trust Gwyn too far if I were you. He did do you a favour by carrying you home, but don't take that for friendship. He's a strange man, one minute he'll help you and then, if it serves his purpose, he'll kill you. Just be careful."

"Are you sure about that? It could just be his reputation is worse through the telling of it," said Caradoc, who liked the thief.

"It could be, but most reputations have a basis in truth. All I am saying is have a care in your dealings with him," advised Ednyfed.

"He does seem to have a soft spot for you but just be careful. Now go and have your mother check that dressing, I can see some blood seeping out."

Caradoc returned to the house and Ednyfed watched Gwyn ride down the road towards the town in the valley. Ednyfed couldn't get it out of his mind that Gwyn had come for something other than to know how Caradoc was doing.

He decided that he would have Owain scout round the farm to ensure that there was no one else spying on them and to make sure that there was no stock missing. One couldn't be too careful, especially when the likes of Gwyn Mochyn were prowling around.

Caersws – Dyfi Valley

Gwyn Mochyn crossed the river Severn at a ford just to the west of Newtown and he rode swiftly along the flat valley floor, following the river up to Caersws. He stopped at The Buck inn and soon established that Iolo had left the village that had once been the capital of the kingdom of Powys in the morning, going up into the mountains as if he were heading for the coast.

Gwyn followed the trail north-west along the river Garno and soon found the place just north of Pontdolgoch where someone had turned from the main track back towards the north-east. *Wild country,* thought Gwyn.

Gwyn dismounted and had a careful look at the tracks that led away from the main road. He could not be sure that the horse belonged to Iolo but if a man was trying to avoid people going cross-country that would certainly be one way of doing it.

The country was wild in the north-west of Montgomeryshire but where Iolo was headed it was the quickest route. Gwyn was thinking he should have brought some supplies with him as he followed Iolo's tracks across some of the wildest country in Wales. Gwyn dismounted occasionally to check the tracks but the rider hadn't disguised them and they followed a clear sheep track over the hills.

He walked his horse as they climbed out of the river valley and up into the mountains. It was getting dark as he recognised the lakes Llyn Du (Black Lake) and Llyn Mawr (Large Lake). He stopped by Llyn Mawr and made a dry camp; he did not make a fire because he didn't want Iolo to know he was being followed. A fire on the hills could be seen for miles.

He hobbled his horse and then let it drink and wander free to graze. The wind from the south-west swept in, making his camp very cold. He found himself a hollow in the ground to shield himself from the biting wind, but the wind still chilled him to his bones.

Gwyn filled his flask with fresh mountain water and he drank his fill, hoping it would stave off his hunger. As the sun dipped below the horizon he wrapped himself in his cloak and tried to get some sleep.

He lay on his back and looked up at the clear skies. The stars were bright and it was almost a full moon, so to keep warm, he decided to use the ambient light to press on. He saddled his horse and started to follow the trail left by Iolo. His progress was slow but at least the exercise kept him warm.

The trail climbed up onto a wide moor land with marshes that could suck a man down where he would never be found. Gwyn stuck to the defined trial, following almost in the very steps Iolo had left only hours before.

As dawn broke he could see the trail leading him down to Afon Rhiw to the village of Llanllugan, a small settlement on the bank of the river by a small church. Here he found the horse he had been following and it did not belong to Iolo. The farmer who owned it was sitting by the river, bathing his feet in the cool water.

As soon as he realised his mistake Gwyn mounted his horse and rode back the way he had come at a canter. He reached Pontdolgoch by mid-morning and turned up the river valley and rode on as he had lost so much time on Iolo.

River Dyfi

Iolo's horse went lame as he reached the river Dyfi. He inspected its hoof and it had a stone embedded in it. He used his knife to extract a stone shard but he knew he would not be able to ride the horse for some time. He walked on but the limping horse was really slowing him down. He needed to hurry on so he could deliver his message.

Iolo spotted a farmhouse where the river Dyfi met a stream running into it. He walked the horse over to the farmhouse and knocked on the door. Two dogs came rushing round the side of the house and the horse shied away from them. As Iolo got his horse under control the farmer came out to see what all the commotion was about.

He shooed the dogs away and turned to Iolo. "What's going on here? What do you want?"

"That's a fine welcome," said Iolo as he stroked the horse's neck to soothe him. "My horse has gone lame and I need another to get me to Bala or Corwen."

"You'll not find a horse for sale around here; the nearest place would be Machynlleth, about seven miles back down the river towards the estuary."

"I have a message to deliver in the north. Where can I get a horse in that direction?, I've lost too much time already," complained Iolo, looking round the farm to see if the farmer had any horses.

"We've no use for horses up here. I hire a ploughman from Machynlleth when I need the fields ploughed but I have my dogs for herding the sheep and I herd them on foot. So if you want a horse you need to go to Machynlleth or start walking."

"Can you look after my horse until I return to get him?" asked Iolo, knowing that the animal would only slow his walking pace.

"You can leave him in the field but I won't have time to look after him so I suggest you come and get him as soon as possible," said the farmer unhelpfully. "If he gets stolen, that's your problem."

Iolo understood the ultimatum but had no other choice but to leave the horse in the farmer's care. Iolo led his horse away to the field beside the farm. He stripped off the saddle and stored it in the farmer's lean-to shed at the end of the farmhouse. Iolo gathered his gear and made a pack from a tarp and some of the horse's harness. He put his arrow bag over his shoulder and with bow in hand he set off at a good pace up the valley.

The sides of the valley got steeper as he walked up it. He knew the terrain and if he continued up the valley he could cross the mountains to the east of Llechwedd Du and this would bring him down to Llyn Tegid (Bala Lake). He followed the river because it was the easiest route and he had already spent too much time covering his tracks in the Vale of Ceri.

Iolo knew the message he bore was important but he did not know what the message was as it had been written in Latin by the lord bishop's cleric. So he strode forward, looking at each farm to see if they had any horses. His first objective was to find a horse. If possible, he would buy it, but if not then he would steal one, even though he would suffer for it if he was caught.

He was making good progress up the valley when the rain started to fall. Soon the track he was following turned into a quagmire and his progress slowed. He cursed his horse for going lame as he toiled his way along the valley, splashing through the mud.

He had been counting his paces to be able to estimate his progress but when the rain came down and it got slippery underfoot he abandoned it. When the sun reached its apex he spotted a farm with a small wood behind it and he knew he was not far from the border with Merioneth. He walked on to the farm, hoping to get some food and shelter before continuing on his journey north. As he reached the farm the rain stopped and the farm door opened. A young woman came out into the yard with a broom in her hand.

Iolo smiled at her and said, "I could do with some warm food if you have some to spare?"

The young woman looked up, startled by his presence. "We've just eaten but if you come in I'm sure my mam can find you something to eat."

"Thank you. Do you know anyone who might sell me a horse or lend me one for a few days so I can get to Llyn Tegid?"

"No," she said, shaking her head, so Iolo followed the young woman into the farmhouse kitchen where a man and woman were sitting at a table on which the remains of a meal were still in evidence.

Iolo introduced himself and repeated his requests for food and for a horse.

"There aren't many horses to spare up here. You might get one in Machynlleth but we mostly travel on foot. We herd sheep on foot with our dogs and share the ploughing in season but a horse is expensive to keep," said the farmer.

The woman got up and ladled some stew into a bowl and set it on the table while the farmer passed Iolo some bread. The younger woman brought him a tankard of beer and then disappeared out of the door with her broom.

Iolo watched her go and then turned his attention to the food before him. He had not realised how hungry he was but he made himself eat the food slowly so that he could absorb some of the heat from the warm room.

He had nearly dozed off to sleep when the farmer said, "If you're prepared for the risk you might go to Gwesty'r Llew Coch (Red Lion inn), in Dinas Mawddwy. Sometimes there's a brigand there who'll have a horse for sale, but it would usually be stolen."

"How far is that?" asked Iolo, suddenly awake.

"About three to four miles, just a good stretch of the legs for a young man like you," said the farmer. "If you start now you should be there before they go back into the hills."

Iolo stood up, stretched and said, "Thank you for the meal, I didn't realise how hungry I was. Thank you."

He picked up his pack and his bow and headed for the door. The farmer joined him and pointed out the best route to travel up the valley, avoiding the marshy ground of the river meadows.

Iolo set out, feeling much better for his meal, and he was soon setting a much better pace than he had in getting to the farm.

River Dyfi

Gwyn Mochyn reached the river Dyfi and stopped to rest his horse which he had ridden hard all morning and into the early afternoon. He studied the tracks on the road to determine which way Iolo had gone. Had he gone west to the coast or north-east up into the mountains?

He took the coast road but soon found the tracks on the road were over a day old and he didn't believe that Iolo was that far ahead of him. So he turned round and rode north along the side of the river.

It was getting towards dusk when he spotted the farmhouse with a horse in the field behind it. Gwyn patted his horse's neck, thinking that he could exchange his horse for a fresh mount and keep riding through the night.

He rode up to the farm and the dogs came scampering round the house into the yard. Gwyn dismounted and led his horse to the water trough and let him drink. He patted the dogs on the head and knocked on the door of the house and waited. It was a few minutes later when the farmer came strolling across the field.

Gwyn hailed him and asked, "Can I borrow your horse and leave mine here to rest?"

"That's what the other fellow wanted but that horse there is lame. He'll be coming back for him but he said he wouldn't be back for a week or so, going somewhere north he was," the farmer volunteered.

Gwyn immediately realised whose horse it was and knew he was not that far behind Iolo, who was now on foot.

Gwyn thanked the farmer and led his weary horse back onto the road going north. He walked alongside his horse but still made a good pace following in Iolo's footsteps. As he walked he looked out for fresh boot tracks and his diligence was rewarded as he found Iolo's boot marks in some soft mud after he had crossed a small stream which flowed down off the mountain. The footprint was fresh, not more than a few hours old; he could tell this from the way the print was still formed and the firmness of the edges which had not yet dried out in the wind.

Gwyn pondered on whether to ride on and try to catch Iolo before nightfall or to make camp and get within sight of him tomorrow. The thought of stopping and resting won so he mounted up and rode on until he came to the farm where Iolo had eaten.

Gwyn rode up to the house and dismounted. He waited for the farmer to come out but when he didn't Gwyn knocked at the door.

The farmer's wife opened it and said, "You're the second visitor we've had today. It's not usual to have so many travellers in a day."

"Can I put my horse in your barn for the night? We've been travelling all day and he's just about done in, and so am I."

"My husband will be back soon, so take care of your horse and he'll see you when he gets back," she said and shut the door firmly.

The only person Glyn could think of that was travelling this way was Iolo. He led his horse over to the barn and removed his saddle and rubbed the horse down with some straw. He forked some hay for the horse and shook out his blankets to make a bed in the next stall. He checked his weapons and the rest of his equipment.

As he straightened up he heard someone behind him. He turned slowly and there was the woman's husband. He was watching Gwyn carefully; he'd noted Gwyn's weapons, the falchion at his hip and the bow leaning on the wall of the stall.

"I see you've made yourself at home?" said the farmer.

"Yes, thanks, better than sleeping out on the moors, which I did last night. At least it's dry and out of the wind. I've used some of your hay for my horse, I hope you don't mind."

The farmer nodded his ascent and said, "We'll be eating in an hour. You're welcome to come and join us when you're ready. I hope you're more talkative than the last one." He left Gwyn currying his horse.

When he finished he went to the house and joined the farmer and his wife at the kitchen table. They were pleased to talk about the traveller who had passed by earlier on foot and Gwyn kept them talking by gently asking questions. He did not want to appear too interested in the traveller but from the way they described him it was obviously Iolo.

Gwyn had a pleasant surprise when the farmer's daughter entered the kitchen and sat down at the table as he had not enjoyed the company of a young woman for some time. As for Iolo before him, with the warmth of the kitchen and the pleasant talk he began to feel his tiredness creep upon him.

Gwyn talked about the weather and brought news of what was happening along the border. The farmer listened carefully, knowing that whatever happened in the Marches usually had an impact on the whole of the principality.

After several tankards of ale Gwyn made his way unsteadily back across the yard to his bed in the hay.

Dinas Mawddwy

Iolo reached The Red Lion at Dinas Mawddwy before the sun had gone down and he entered the bar to see if he could find anyone who would sell him a horse. He approached the bar and ordered a tankard of ale to slake his thirst after his brisk walk.

After making the usual pleasantries he asked the innkeeper, "Is there a horse trader in the village? I have need of a horse to get me to Llyn Tegid."

"Madoc Mawr might have one but he's not in a good mood. Be better if you spoke to him in the morning."

"Where would I find him?" Iolo persisted.

"He'll be with his horses at the paddock at the other end of the village. He's mad because he's just had a horse stolen by the brigands and it was one of his favourites."

"What happened?" enquired Iolo, wanting to know what had happened. He did not want to annoy the horse trader by making untoward remarks, especially as he seemed to be the only one who could supply him with the horse he needed.

"He left his horses in his paddock as usual when he went to check on his sheep up on the hill and when he got back, his stallion was missing. He's had that horse since it was a foal. He hand reared it and was going to use it to breed," said the landlord. "So at the moment he's inconsolable."

"Do you have any idea who might have taken it?" asked Iolo.

"Everyone knows who's got it," answered the landlord with a laugh that Iolo did not care for.

"Then why doesn't he go and get it back?"

"Ah! Now there's the problem," said the landlord cryptically. "The person who took it is the rightful owner."

"But I thought you just said Madoc reared the horse from a foal and it was stolen by brigands."

"Yes, well the brigand in question is Madoc's brother Eirian and he owned the mare that had the stallion, so the horse is rightfully his. Madoc didn't think his brother would come back for it when he took the stallion from their father's farm, so there you have the dilemma."

"Where's the dilemma if the horse is with its rightful owner?"

"As Madoc see it, he's the one who reared and trained it and now his brother will get the benefit of a saddle trained horse, and a good stallion which can be bred from at that. So he's not a happy man. He'll probably just turn your request for a horse down out of hand. Whereas if you ask him in the morning when he's sobered up you might get a better answer. Do you want a room for the night?" asked the landlord.

Iolo instantly realised from the question that the landlord of The Red Lion was just trying to get him to rent a room. "I'll wait for the moment, thank you."

"Suit yourself but the rooms could be all taken if you don't book one soon."

Iolo look round the empty bar and said, "I'll take my chances." He drained his tankard and went off to see if he could find Madoc Mawr.

Iolo found ostler in the paddock inspecting the hooves of one of his horses, a fine grey mare.

Iolo leaned on the gate and said, "I'm looking for a horse to get me to Bala."

Madoc looked up. "Rent or buy?"

"Rent if possible, buy if necessary," Iolo replied as he tried to size up the horse trader.

"When do you need it? I have a horse being returned tomorrow morning I can let you have."

"I was hoping to be on my way tonight, but I can wait until tomorrow if necessary. I want to be travelling as soon as possible."

"That's a hard trail to ride at night and I wouldn't want one of my horses riding over those mountains in the dark, it's an easy way to get a horse to break a leg."

"Tomorrow it is then," said Iolo as he resigned himself to staying in the village for the night. He remembered what the landlord had said about the stallion and asked, "The landlord said you'd lost a stallion to a thief."

Madoc straightened and his face clouded over. "Running off at the mouth again is he? He knows that horse belongs to my brother Eirian and he's always trying to stir up trouble for him."

"Am I missing something here?" asked Iolo, surprised at Madoc's reaction.

"Rhodri's always had it in for my brother ever since he beat him soundly in a horse race. He's the only one who calls my brother an outlaw and he tells that to every traveller passing through. I suppose he also wanted you to stay the night at his inn?"

"He did offer me a room, yes," replied Iolo.

Madoc gave a big sigh and then Iolo saw him relax and the anger drain from him. He waved Iolo to join him, "I have a place in the stables with the horses if you want it; you'll be here then when my horse comes in. She's a good horse and she knows the way to Bala. She's only coming a couple of miles, so she'll be fresh to travel. Do you need a saddle as well?"

"Yes, I left mine with my horse when he went lame. He's back down the valley at a farm by the river. Do you think you could bring him here and have a look at his hoof?" asked Iolo as he could see the man had an affinity with horses and could probably help his horse to recover faster than if it was just left at the farm.

"I'll see what I can do but if he's lame it might be better to leave him where he is until he's healed, but I can go and have a look at him for you," said Madoc.

"He had a stone shard in his hoof and now he's limping badly."

The two men fell into an easy silence as they made their way into the barn to prepare a bed for Iolo for the night.

Dinas Mawddwy

Gwyn Mochyn was up before dawn and had his horse saddled before the farmer came out to invite him into the kitchen for breakfast. The rain had stopped so he was keen to get on his way to catch up with Iolo before he left the inn in Dinas Mawddwy.

"I must get moving if I'm to reach my destination before nightfall," Gwyn made his excuses.

The farmer went back into the kitchen and returned with some bread and cheese for Gwyn to eat as he rode. Gwyn thanked the man and set off down the road at a canter. He wanted to get to The Red Lion before he lost Iolo again.

Gwyn covered the five miles between the farm and the village in good time and arrived at The Red Lion before Rhodri, the landlord, had roused the men who were sleeping in the bar for the night. He put his horse in the stable and found it some grain for its nosebag. He rubbed the horse down and re-saddled him so he was ready to leave at a moment's notice.

Gwyn entered the bar and scanned the room to see if he could locate Iolo. He was not happy when the other man did not appear to be at the inn. He did not want to raise any suspicions so he walked to the bar and asked if they were serving breakfast.

The barmaid drew him a tankard of small beer and he went to sit by the fire to wait for the bread and meat promised. The warmth of the fire warmed him and his spirits rose as he looked out of the window to see the mist rising over the river.

He got up and asked the landlord, "If I wanted to buy a horse, who would I talk to?"

"You're the second fellow to ask that question in two days," said the landlord and he went into his story about Eirian, Madoc's brother, and by the time he had finished Gwyn knew where Iolo was waiting.

The food arrived and Gwyn was able to relax while he ate, secure in the knowledge that Iolo would have to ride past the inn to join the road for Bala which was the direction he seemed to be heading in.

As the morning wore on Gwyn became concerned that he had missed Iolo so he walked out and looked at the tracks on the road. Several men had left the inn and had taken this road along the river Dyfi going north-east. He went to the stables and checked his horse. He nearly missed Iolo as he trotted past as Gwyn came out of the stables. He walked into the road and looked carefully at the horse's hoof prints so that he would recognise them on the road. The horse's front shoe left a distinctive print.

Gwyn bought some supplies and loaded them in a pack behind his saddle. He cursed Rory for sending him on this wild goose chase. He had not expected to have to travel so far. He waited until Iolo was out of sight before he began to follow him. Before he mounted his horse he strung his bow because he was heading into what for him was unknown territory. He held his bow across his saddle ready for use.

Gwyn rode slowly following the tracks left by Iolo. He occasionally glimpsed his quarry in the distance but did not make any effort to catch him up. The information he needed was who the message was being delivered to, so all he had to do was follow Iolo, not catch him. He kept a steady pace because he didn't want to tire his horse.

Dinas Mawddwy – Bala

Madoc's horse arrived later than he expected and so Iolo was late in setting out. Madoc loaned him a saddle as well as an old pack to carry his belongings in behind the saddle. While he was waiting Iolo bought some supplies and was ready to be off as soon as the farmer who had been using the horse arrived.

Iolo had time to walk around the village and he noted the various men who seemed to be hanging around for no purpose. He sharpened his falchion and strung his bow. He did not like riding with his bow across his saddle but he was also aware of the area's reputation for brigands and outlaws. This was truly wild Wales and the valley he was riding up would be a natural place for an ambush.

When the horse arrived he rubbed it down and fed it some oats before saddling it and preparing for the road.

He ate some of his rations and then set off, riding through the village and north along the side of the river. Every mile or so he would turn in his saddle and watch his back trail to see if he was being followed. It was just a precaution but he had an uneasy feeling that he was being watched. He wished he had not talked to Rhodri, the landlord of The Red Lion; he didn't trust the man after what Madoc had said about him.

Iolo made steady progress through the day with the steep mountains on either side of the valley. He passed some remote farms that were built on the steep slopes of the mountains but he did not stop as he knew that time was of the essence. Upwards he rode into the mountains and he followed a tributary up past some cliffs and on towards the top of a mountain called Moel y Cerrig Duon. From this height he could see down the valley of Afon Twrch which flowed into the south-western end of Lake Bala. It was a splendid view but the wind from the south-west was bitterly cold, so he pulled his cloak about him and rode down into the shelter of the river's valley.

Iolo was so intent on gaining some cover from the wind that he did not notice the man observing him from a small wood that ran along the eastern side of the valley. The man stood very still so that no movement attracted his quarry's attention.

Iolo rode on as the sun was beginning to dip in the west. The sun was like a great red ball, and Iolo felt as if he could reach out and pluck it from the sky.

It was more luck than judgement that saved him from the archer's arrow. He had stopped to let the horse have a drink from the stream and he was just dismounting as the arrow came from the small wood to the east. Iolo swung down as the arrow flashed by his cheek. He threw himself backwards onto the ground and then bounced straight back up onto his feet. He grabbed his arrow bag from the horse and jumped away from the horse, looking for some cover.

Two more arrows landed where he had fallen and Iolo was unable to spot where they had come from. He ran away from the horse and found a bank to hide behind. He nocked an arrow to his bow and waited for one of his attackers to show himself.

The waiting tried his patience but eventually a man appeared in the tree line and fired an arrow. Iolo stood up and shot back. The arrow slammed into the man, wounding him, but a shower of arrows came back at him so Iolo had to dive back behind the bank for cover. Now he knew he was outnumbered and in a vulnerable position.

He knew he was pinned down and that he would have to wait for dark to escape, if they didn't charge him first. The ambusher's changed their tactics and started to move forward, some men shooting to give covering fire which pinned Iolo behind his bank as others crept forward. He managed to get another shot off at the bowmen in the trees but the men with falchions and spears were slowly surrounding him.

Iolo pulled his falchion from his belt and made ready to fight for his life. The bushwhackers were slowing encircling him at the water's edge and Iolo knew he didn't stand a chance against so many. Five men were coming forward and that still left the archers who were still hidden in the trees. He drew back his bow and let fly at almost arm's length. The arrow went straight through the man and he fell onto his back, writhing in pain. The other men rushed forward and Iolo dropped his bow and swung his falchion in a defensive arc to keep the man at arm's length.

Iolo backed away deeper into the river when an arrow thudded into one of his attackers. The arrow slammed into the man's face, killing him instantly. The three remaining men looked around and the nearest one lunged forward at Iolo. Iolo parried the blow and stabbed the man in the eye with his poniard. He withdrew the blade and struggled to get back to the river bank, away from the other attackers. The two remaining swordsmen moved in to renew their attack. Iolo charged at one and an arrow took the other in the throat. The wounded man was driven backwards by the force of the arrow but it did not kill him. Blood poured from the wound in his neck and he still struggled to find his feet. A third arrow thudded home into the man's face, knocking him onto his back, dead.

Iolo managed to stay clear of his attacker until he could get his feet onto some solid ground. The man came on, driving Iolo backwards with powerful swipes of his sword. Iolo feinted and then spun round, dropping his poniard and swinging his falchion with both hands, slicing through his attacker's head. The falchion hit the man's head at the temple on the right side and cut through flesh and bone, exiting from the man's face and taking a good part of the man's jaw with it. Blood and saliva poured from the man's face and wash washed away in the current of the stream.

Iolo spun again and this time he brought the falchion down on the man's collarbone which shattered under the blow. The falchion sliced into the man, driving deep into his chest. Blood poured into the river and it took Iolo a great deal of effort to work his falchion free of the dead body.

Iolo looked round to see if there were any more attackers but the men in the trees had melted away. He dipped his falchion into the water and washed the blood and gore from the blade. He picked up his poniard and slid it back into its sheath, keeping his eye on the tree line where he thought the archers were still lurking. He slid the dead man's sword into his belt; it was a good weapon and too good to just discard.

Iolo started towards his bow when he became aware of a horseman on the knoll on the western side of the river. He looked up at the man but did not recognise him. The man held a bow with a nocked arrow and was watching the forest on the eastern bank.

"Your horse has run north, I'll go and get him. You keep a watch for those bowmen in the woods, they can't have gone very far," said the horseman. He pulled on his reins and rode after Iolo's horse.

Iolo hooked his falchion to his belt and gathered up his bow and arrow bag. As he passed the body of one of the fallen men he scooped up the man's belt pouch and attached it to his belt. He nocked an arrow and moved north towards the horseman who had saved his life. The bowmen in the trees did not reappear so Iolo walked north, keeping close to the river. The horseman returned with Iolo's horse and brought it so Iolo could mount with the horse between him and the woods where the remainder of the ambushers were hidden.

As soon as Iolo was in the saddle both men rode north at the gallop until they were clear of the forest. They slowed their horses to a brisk walk but kept a careful watch for any other travellers.

Iolo turned to Gwyn and said, "Thank you, I thought I was a dead man, they had me pinned down in the river. Do you know who they are?"

Gwyn shook his head, "No, I saw them attack you as you got down to the valley floor. It was self-preservation. I attacked them because they would have killed me after they killed you, so it was in my interests to get them before they got me. You provided a good distraction for me to come up on them unnoticed."

Iolo took the explanation and said, "Well, I'm still in your debt."

Gwyn led the way and they rode swiftly down the valley until they reached the village at the southern edge of Lake Bala. They did not stop but skirted the village and continued on their way along the southern edge of the lake. They slowed up as they trotted along at a good pace. Iolo watched his new companion and was suspicious that he had turned up just at the right time. *Was he one of the outlaws who had attacked him? No! He killed at least two of them.* But Iolo's suspicion still lingered in his mind.

The going was good and they made directly for the village of Bala at the north-eastern edge of the lake.

Gwyn introduced himself as soon as they slowed down. "I'm just travelling to get away from my mother-in-law who makes my wife behave like a shrew. Once she's gone home I can do the same. I'm also looking for some horses but I doubt I'll find what I'm looking for up here, I may have to go south to Brecon or even down as far as Gloucester."

"What do you need the horses for?" asked Iolo, making conversation with his companion.

"Lord Rhys, he breeds them. His lordship had some of his horses stolen a few weeks ago so he needs to replace the stock," Gwyn lied easily.

"I know him, we met at a farm just south of Newtown. He seems to be a friend of the Mortimers," said Iolo, digging for information about the Welsh aristocrat.

"Self-preservation more like. He plays one off against another; it's how he keeps his lands despite the English laws," said Gwyn. "He's very shrewd about his dealings with the marcher lords. He keeps them on the other side of Offa's Dyke but they are making inroads up the Severn Valley at Newtown. We've been losing ground ever since the Mortimers took over running the castle at Dolforwyn."

"You sound as if you admire him," said Iolo, watching Gwyn's reaction.

"I respect him and occasionally I work for him so I suppose I have a vested interest," grinned Gwyn. "What about you, why are you travelling such dangerous roads?"

"Just making my way home to Corwen. My lord is a squire to the Earl of Arundel; he's also a lawyer, trained at the Inns of Court in London. He's an important man and his ancestors were Princes of Powys."

"Every lord I've met has ancestors who were once princes," grinned Gwyn at his companion.

"With Owain ap Gruffydd Fychan it's true. He's a real gentleman but he also has troubles with the marcher lords who are greedy for estates and land, and the worst is Lord de Grey of Ruthin. The man is never satisfied. He now has the ear of the king since helping him onto the throne so we will have even more trouble from now on," Iolo explained. "Lord Grey wants to take over as much of Wales as he can get his hands on, and that will not be good for our people."

"What will your Lord Owain do about it?" asked Gwyn, curious to know more about this Welsh princeling. *If Iolo worked for this prince what was he doing at Ednyfed's farm in the Severn Valley?*

"Owain supported the king on his last campaign to Scotland but his influence has diminished since the old Earl of Arundel died last year. He's now trying to gain what support he can from the new Earl of Arundel and his uncle, the Archbishop of Canterbury. But the archbishop is newly reinstated to his See and the new earl does not have the strength or influence his father had."

Gwyn listened to Iolo explain how Owain had tried to comply with the king's demands but how it was getting more and more difficult with Lord de Grey agitating the king against him.

"You do know we have the king's son, Henry of Monmouth, as the Prince of Wales. He's trying to extend his control of Wales from the castles at Chester and Ludlow," Iolo explained.

Gwyn laughed and said, "Did anyone tell our people? They barely let our own lords rule over them; they certainly won't let some foreigner rule. He can come into the mountains but all he'll find is water, rocks and grass and while he's out there we'll steal him blind."

Iolo said sternly, "They're already using Edward's castles and they are building more. They'll hold the castles and the towns and we'll hold the country. What we have to do is to take back the castles with their adjoining towns and push them out of Wales altogether."

The village of Bala came into sight in the dim distance and Gwyn said, "I hope you know a good inn because I'm starving, I could eat a horse."

Iolo answered, "I know the landlord at the inn but this is an example of the invasion of the English. Roger de Mortimer got a Royal Charter to hold a market in the Bala eighty years ago. The only reason he did it was to have a garrison there to get at the rebels in Penllyn."

"Did he succeed in catching the rebels?"

"Not really, they took the village but the rebels just vanished into the mountains. The English haven't a clue how to deal with us when we won't stand and give them a pitched battle."

"Do you have to turn every question into an argument against the English? All I want is something to eat and a bed for the night," Gwyn said as he adjusted himself in his saddle. He stopped his horse and dismounted. "I think I need to walk for a while, I'm getting stiff in the saddle."

Iolo dismounted and they walked to the bridge to cross the river to enter the village of Bala.

Bala, Clyn Tegid (Bala Cake)

Gwyn followed Iolo along the only street of the village to the inn. They stabled their horses, leaving them with a stable boy to care for them. Iolo entered the inn and went directly to the bar. Gwyn followed but stood by the doorway until he had surveyed the room. He let his eyes adjust to the dim light of the bar. His eyes flicked over every man in the room and he measured the threat posed by each one.

It was only when Iolo was talking to the landlord of the inn that Gwyn noticed he was carrying a sword as well as the falchion he had seen him wielding at the riverside. From where he stood he could see that it was a good weapon and one probably imported from over the border. He must have picked it up from the fight, Gwyn surmised.

The landlord placed two tankards on the bar and Iolo called him over. Gwyn walked over to the bar and was introduced to the landlord called Huw.

"I hear you had an eventful journey," said the landlord.

"I've had more peaceful rides," Gwyn replied, feeling tried all of a sudden. He did not want to spend his time in idle chit chat, but inns were a good place to find out what was happening the area.

Huw returned his attention back to Iolo. "You missed him by a few hours. I'd wait until morning and you should catch him when he gets back to Glyndyfrdwy."

Iolo nodded. "What have you got that's edible because my friend is starving and I owe him a good meal at the very least."

"I've a lamb roasting but don't ask where it came from. Find yourselves a table and I'll have Eleri bring it over."

They found a table near the window and Gwyn sat down. Iolo tried to sit down but had trouble with his weapons. He unhooked his falchion and drew the sword from his belt and propped them against the wall and sat down in his chair. He took his eating knife from his pouch and waited for the food to arrive.

Eleri soon delivered two trenchers of roast lamb with vegetables and they both ate with good appetite. It was only as they were finishing their meal that Gwyn noticed that a man at a table near the door was eying them curiously. Eventually the man stood up and came over and stood over Iolo. Iolo looked up at the man questioningly.

"Where did you get that sword?" demanded the man as he moved towards Iolo.

"Why, would you like to buy it?" asked Iolo flippantly. He knew he had said the wrong thing as soon as the words were out of his mouth. He moved his chair so that he was closer to the sword and falchion.

"No, but I know the man you stole it from," came the sharp reply.

"I took this from a bastard who tried to kill me with it," Iolo snapped back.

Iolo came out of his chair and drove his head into the man's chest as he rose. He stretched out his hand, grasping his falchion as he left the chair. The other man staggered back as Iolo straightened up to his full height. He held his falchion in front of him, ready to defend himself.

The man regained his balance and said, "You're a liar. My brother wouldn't attack anyone except in self-defence."

"Sior, I know this man," said the landlord, "and I'll have no fighting in my inn. He's one of Owain ap Gruffydd's men and I'll have him treated with respect."

"I don't care who he is, that's my brother's sword," said Sior, not placated.

"I took it off the body of an outlaw who attacked me as I was riding down the valley on my way towards the lake. The man who had this sword attacked me with four others and now they're all dead."

"You killed five men on your own?" demanded the man, unbelieving that one man could kill so many on his own.

"No, fortunately my companion here came and saved me from the men who laid the ambush for me. Who are you, the brother of an outlaw?" said Iolo, who was beginning to get angry.

Sior glanced at Gwyn and saw that he too had a weapon in his hand and had moved his chair so that he could be on his feet in an instant and ready to fight.

"I'm no outlaw and my brother wouldn't do that. You're a liar, Sion's no thief. You know that, don't you, Huw?" said Sior, raising his voice, which attracted the attention of the rest of the customers in the inn. He had challenged one man but could now see he was faced with two and he could not judge which side the landlord would take.

"I'd have said that once, Sior, but he's changed since he lost his farm," said Huw, not knowing how to deal with the situation. He wanted to placate both men because he didn't want his inn wrecked with a brawl.

"When did your brother lose his farm?" asked Iolo, now interested in what Sior had to say.

"About a month ago," answered Sior, who had not expected to be asked such a question. He concentrated on the sword when Iolo asked another question.

"Who took his farm away?"

"De Grey's men threw him out of the farm my father had and his father before him. He tried to get justice from the prince in Chester but he wouldn't even hear him," said the distraught man.

"That's true enough," said Huw, "but I don't see what Iolo can do about it, your real quarrel is with de Grey."

"I'm going to see Lord Owain. I think you should come with me and tell him about what happened to your brother," said Iolo. "I think he would like to hear what you have to say about de Grey's stewardship of his lands."

"What about my brother's sword?" asked Sior.

Iolo leaned his falchion against the wall and picked up the sword. He weighed it in his and then reversed the pommel toward Sior. "I'm sorry about your brother. You'd better send some men to take care of the bodies. We had no time to bury them."

Sior took the sword and put the point on the ground. "I'll take care of it myself. I'll catch up with you on the road to Glyndyfrdwy."

Sior move towards the door and several men who had been sitting with him finished their drinks and followed him out into the night.

Huw breathed a huge sigh of relief. "Thank God, I thought I was going to have some real trouble. I can do without a brawl, the place gets wrecked and no one ever has any money to pay for the repairs."

Iolo smiled, "All the more evidence to persuade Lord Owain that the English are not going to leave us alone to manage our own affairs."

Huw started to clear the table that Sior and his men had just vacated. He took the tankards back to the bar and then wiped the table with a cloth.

Gwyn, who had been silent through the whole confrontation, said, "Are you sure you want to meet him on the road? I think we'd better leave early and get to your Lord Owain before Sior has time to catch us on the open road. We are only two and we don't know how many archers were hidden in those woods."

Huw, who overheard Gwyn's comment, said, "Why not rest for a couple of hours and then ride on so that you can be at Lord Owain's estate at daybreak."

Gwyn cleaned his plate and handed it to Huw, "You may have a point there. Can you have your stable lad check that Sior and his men have left the village and which road they took?"

Huw took the platter away and went to find the stable boy.

Iolo looked at Gwyn, "Why? Do you really think he'll attack us?"

"He could have been one the bowmen in the woods, and you didn't ask him how he identified his brother's sword. You also let him know which way you would be travelling," said Gwyn as he eased his poniard back into its sheath.

"I thought you would be coming with me to meet Lord Owain," said Iolo. He had not considered that Gwyn would choose another route.

"I'll travel with you but let's see if we can buy two more horses, that way we can ride harder than our pursuers."

Iolo nodded and went to see if the landlord had any horses for sale. Gwyn covered his head with his hood and slumped into his seat to try and get a few minutes' sleep while he could.

Bala – Berwyn Mountains – Glyndyfrdwy

Gwyn woke with a start. He was still sitting in the chair in the bar. He looked around and the bar had one or two others sleeping like himself. The room smelled of wood smoke and stale ale. The fire in the hearth was burning low and there was no one serving behind the bar. Gwyn wiped his face with his hands and rubbed the sleep from his eyes.

Iolo was nowhere to be seen, so Gwyn quietly eased himself up from his chair and stretched. His one leg had pins and needles so he stamped his foot on the floor until the feeling came back. He walked over to the hearth and stirred the ashes with a poker. Some embers glowed so he added some small sticks to the fire and soon the new wood was blazing. He added some more fuel and could feel the increase in heat in the room.

He gathered his gear together and thought about going out to find his horse so he would be ready to go at first light. He checked his bow and counted his supply of arrows. He tested the edge on his falchion and made sure all his knives were where he expected them to be.

He noticed that Iolo's falchion was still leaning against the wall and his arrow bag was on the floor next to his unstrung bow. *He can't have gone far*, thought Gwyn as he eased his poniard in its scabbard. He checked his falchion and then went in search of his travelling companion.

He checked the other travellers and all were sleeping heavily, so he made his way through to the kitchen. There he found Iolo sleeping with his head resting on his hands on the kitchen table. Gwyn looked around to see who else was in the kitchen but he found nobody. Gwyn left Iolo sleeping and returned to the bar where he gathered all their weapons and gear and carried it through to the kitchen. He poured himself a drink of milk and drank it down and then poured another.

He shook Iolo wake. The man was groggy and moaned about being woken. Gwyn did not listen to Iolo's complaints about being woken. He went to the larder and brought out some bread, butter and meat. He placed them on the table and cut himself some meat and tore off a chunk of coarse bread on which he smeared a generous dollop of butter.

Iolo looked at him across the table. "It's still dark."

"That's the whole point, we want to be on the road and gone before the sun is up. We don't want anyone to see us leave. I brought your things through from the bar, so let's get moving."

Gwyn stood up and threw his cloak around his shoulders. "I'll go and saddle the horses. I take it you weren't able to buy any spares?" Iolo shook his head. "Eat something and then we'll be on our way."

Gwyn picked up his arrow bag and his bow and left by the kitchen door to go out to the stables. Gwyn looked about and made sure no one was watching before he crossed the yard to the stables. He peered inside to make sure the stables were empty before entering.

In the kitchen Iolo groaned, but he got to his feet and splashed some water onto his face. He helped himself to a slice of meat, put it in his mouth and started to chew. He considered what Gwyn had said and realised that even though he was close to home he still had a duty to get to Lord Owain. Gwyn was right, the earlier they left the better and anyone watching would probably not be as awake as they should be which would allow their escape.

He armed himself with his weapons and taking some food with him he headed for the stables. Just as he got to the door he had an afterthought and he took some coins from his pouch and left them on the table for Huw.

It was then that he noticed he still had the pouch he had taken from his attacker by the river, Sior's brother. He opened the pouch and looked inside. There were the usual things, bowstrings, twine and some arrowheads, mainly bodkins. But at the bottom there were five gold florins. The find was totally unexpected. *Where would an outlaw get such a sum?*

The ambush was premeditated. The realisation struck home like a poleaxe. A Welshman could only have been given such coins by an Englishman and a rich one at that. Someone like Lord de Grey. He closed the pouch and hurried out to the stables.

Gwyn had his horse saddled with his bow strung and his arrow bag hanging where he could draw his arrows quickly. Gwyn was saddling Iolo's horse when he heard Iolo enter the stables behind him. He turned and could see something was wrong from Iolo's expression.

"What's wrong?" Gwyn asked.

"They were waiting for me. This pouch came from Sior's brother and it has five gold florins in it and the only place a man like him would get this sort of cash would be from an English lord."

"Can I see?"

Iolo showed Gwyn the coins, and Gwyn took one and turned it over in his hand. He bit it and nodded. "I've never seen one of these before." He handed it back to Iolo. "What do you want to do?"

"Get back to Corwen or Glyndyfrdwy as soon as possible."

"Have you seen Huw this morning?"

"No."

"Do you think he's involved?" asked Iolo, now becoming suspicious of everyone.

"I don't know but if he is he won't want our deaths linked to his inn," said Gwyn, "As soon as we leave Bala we'll be vulnerable and I think Sior and his men are out there just waiting for us."

Gwyn continued, "They'll expect us to follow the river Dyfrdwy because it takes us directly along the valley to Lord Owain's estate, and it's fairly flat. I think we should head east into the Berwyn mountains. We'll be harder to follow."

"That means crossing the river; we'll be exposed on the bridge."

"I don't think they'll attack us so close to the village, especially if Huw's involved. Look at where they attacked last time. They had plenty of cover to slip away. There's a flat plain where the river flows out of the lake so we ride now and get over the river before the sun rises and then we head east. We go as fast as we can for an hour and then walk the horses so that they are rested if we need to make a run for it. If we leave now we should have surprise on our side and we should get into the hills before they know we've gone."

Iolo loaded his gear onto his horse.

"Did you ask Huw about spare horses?" asked Gwyn as an afterthought. There were several other horses in the stables but they did not know who owned them.

"I asked but he was non-committal, he said he'd ask around in the morning."

"Sounds like another delaying tactic. Let's go."

Gwyn led the way forward and opened the stable doors. They led their horses out into the street and mounted. Gwyn pushed the door closed with his foot and they rode at a slow trot towards the bridge they had crossed only a few hours before.

Once they were over the bridge they rode east to Pont Ceunant, crossing the stream. The trail led south-east into the mountains and was steep, but they pushed their horses on, keen to put as much distance between themselves and Bala as possible. They rode onward and upward, skirting a remote farm and on into the cover of some woods. Here they dismounted to follow a deer track through the thick forest.

The sun was coming up in the east as they came out of the woods. They could see some more woods just about a mile away so they mounted and rode as quickly as they could across the open ground, hoping not to be seen.

"How long do you think it will be before they discover we've gone?" asked Gwyn.

"Any time now, I should think. Eleri will be going into the bar to rouse the guests. It depends on how soon she tells Huw."

"We could be doing him a disservice; he might not be involved at all."

"Better to be safe than sorry. We can't afford to let our guard down until we're clear to Corwen or with Lord Owain in Glyndyfrdwy."

They rode round the southern edge of the woods this time rather than going through them. So far they had seen no one but they could not rely on not having been seen leaving Bala. Sior would probably have left someone to watch the inn.

They were soon skirting round a mountain to their south. They continued east as the sun came up and caught them in the eyes. They shielded their eyes as best they could and continued to climb higher into the Berwyn mountains. A cutting wind blew from the south-east as they passed a cairn set on the side of the mountain. They let their horses drink at a small stream which ran down the hillside to join one of the tributaries of the river Dyfrdwy.

When they got to the main tributary they dismounted and walked with their horses down a steep tree-covered slope to the stream.

"Keep going. We'll head for the cairns at Cadair Berwyn; we'll have an excellent view from there. We can follow the ridge to Cadair Bronwen. The going will be hard until we reach the ridge but then we can take it easy as we head directly for Glyndyfrdwy," said Iolo, who knew the mountains of northern Montgomeryshire well. This was the wild country that was difficult to travel unless you knew what you were doing and which paths to follow.

"If we go too high they'll spot us on the skyline," commented Gwyn, who was not anxious to be caught in open country. Especially country that he did not know well. If he had been in Radnorshire he would have been happier.

"If they come we'll see them in plenty of time to get away. And if we have to fight we'll have a height advantage. We'll be able to pick them off before they get near us."

Gwyn asked cynically, "How many arrows have you got left?"

Iolo looked in his arrow bag and counted, "A score and seven."

"I've a sheaf in my quiver and a score in my arrow bag. That's not going to hold off a concerted attack. And we don't know how many men they have hunting us."

Iolo turned in his saddle and looked into Gwyn's eyes. "This isn't your fight. I'll understand if you want to leave and ride south. You could easily make it to Llangynog."

Gwyn Mochyn laughed. "I saved your skinny arse once, I suppose I'll just have to do it again, and I'd rather like to meet this princeling you put so much faith in."

"Well, if you're sure, I can introduce you for certes," said Iolo with a wicked grin, pleased that Gwyn would remain as his travel companion. He knew that he would not have survived that last ambush if it hadn't been for Gwyn.

It took them until midday to reach Cadair Berwyn, below a rocky outcrop, and they took shelter by a cairn where they ate some of the bread and cheese they had brought with them from Huw's kitchen.

The view over the mountains was spectacular but the wind from the south-west was cutting. They were thankful that the rain had held off but some ominous clouds were scudding in on the wind. The sun was in the south now and shielded by the clouds.

From their vantage point they could see right down the river valley and they could see two groups of men travelling hard north-east along the river valley. The small village of Llandrillo was just three miles down in the bottom of the valley but the climb to their eyrie was about two thousand feet. The leading group were on horseback with the following group on foot.

"I think they've discovered we've gone," said Gwyn stating the obvious. "How many of them do you think there are?"

"About ten horsemen in that leading group and about half as many again in the following group on foot."

"Five-and-twenty men, someone means business, especially if he paid them all in gold florins. Someone must really want you dead. Why?" asked Gwyn bluntly.

"I suppose it won't do any harm to tell you. I'm carrying a message from John Trefor, the Bishop of St Asaph, for Lord Owain of Glyndyfrdwy," confessed Iolo.

"It must be important then, so we'd better get moving even if we only walk with the horses along this track. They have further to go but we've got rougher terrain. Come on." Gwyn got up and led the way along the track beneath the craggy ridge and Iolo followed him. Iolo was pleased with Gwyn's reaction but was unsure about how he could repay his companion. *If we get through to Lord Owain I'll ask him to reward Gwyn in some way,* he thought as he followed Gwyn along the narrow track.

They made good time even though the terrain was rough so that they reached Cadair Bronwen in less than an hour. They crossed a height called Bwrdd Arthur and then it was all downhill to the track crossing at Meml. The track allowed them to mount their horses and trot in single file to the crossing.

They could still see the two groups of men making their way along the river valley. The leading group of horsemen were approaching the village of Corwen several miles ahead of the men on foot who seemed to have slowed their pace.

Iolo and Gwyn could see their next target of Moel Fferna. "We'll be able to see Glyndyfrdwy from there. The men on foot aren't keeping up so that improves the odds."

"Our friends are making good progress along the valley; they'll get there before we do and the odds are still five to one," said Gwyn as he estimated the distances.

"Lord Owain's estate is that moated manor house directly north of Moel Fferna. If we can get into the woods south of the river we should be able to slip onto the estate without being seen."

"And what sort of reception will we get from his lordship?" asked Gwyn, curious to know more about Lord Owain.

"A warm one, I hope," answered Iolo as he urged his horse on towards the cairn at Moel Fferna. They could not ride at full speed down the mountain for fear of breaking a horse's leg. The race was on and they kept up their pace steady and they soon past the cairn and continued down the hill towards the woods. They hoped they had not been spotted by the men who were racing along the valley.

The scenery was beautiful but neither man had time to appreciate it as they raced their horses as the land flattened towards the woods. Iolo slowed his horse as they entered the woods and he led Gwyn onto a broad pathway which threaded through the forest. They were within a mile of the manor when a man stepped out from behind a tree and raised a bow. Iolo charged him, using his horse as a weapon. The man loosed his arrow too soon and it flew harmlessly away into the woods as he dived away from the speeding horsemen. By the time the archer had gained his feet the two riders were out of sight.

He picked up his bow and ran after them, but he had no chance of catching them.

The man stopped and took a horn from his belt and blew a warning. Iolo rode on but Gwyn hung back. Gwyn nocked an arrow and waited for the ambusher to appear along the track. As he came into sight Gwyn shot him in the chest. Not waiting to see the damage his arrow had caused, he wheeled his horse and followed Iolo towards the manor house.

Men raced along the valley to prevent the two fugitives from getting to the manor. The sounding of the horn and the arrival of the horsemen attracted the attention of some of Lord Owain's men who thought that the manor was under attack.

Lord Owain's men armed themselves and made ready to fight but the riders veered away from the manor and charged into the woods. They formed a skirmish line to stop Iolo and Gwyn getting to the Lord Owain's manor.

Iolo slowed as the manor came into sight. He could see the riders through the thinning trees. Gwyn drew abreast of him and said, "I'll lead, if I go down just ride for the manor while I hold them off."

Iolo didn't waste his breath in arguing. He put his spurs to his horse to encourage it to extra speed.

They rode forward, bursting out of the woods onto the floor of the valley. They nearly made it to the river before the first flight of arrows rained down on them. Gwyn wheeled his horse as Iolo rushed on past and into the moat. He leaped from the saddle onto dry land and ran forward towards the safety of the manor house.

Two horsemen came out of the woods and Gwyn met them head on, swinging his falchion right and left as he drove them back with the ferociousness of his attack. One man went down with a deep cut to his shoulder while the other horseman wheeled to try and pierce Gwyn's defence. Gwyn saw the danger too late. The horseman's blade cut him through his jupon along the ribs with a thrust. Gwyn forced himself to rise in his stirrups and swing his falchion with a mighty blow down onto his attacker's head. The man's head split like a melon and blood and brains splattered everywhere. Gwyn sank back into his saddle, blood pouring from his side. He wheeled his horse and cantered slowly towards the manor. Gwyn swayed in the saddle but he held on to his falchion as he held his arm against his wound to staunch the blood loss.

More men came out of the forest; several had bows. Gwyn flattened himself against the neck of his horse and kept riding as arrows flew over his head.

As Iolo reached the manor, Owain's men came out and formed a line with bows ready. The hunters were now the hunted and they retreated back into the woods, leaving the two horsemen to their fate. Gwyn struggled to get his horse under control and then trotted slowly to the entrance of the manor house.

Lord Owain, in full armour, was in command and Iolo was standing beside him as Gwyn slipped from the saddle and landed at their feet in a bloody pile. He tried to get up but his wounds caused him to collapse and pass out. The defenders ignored him until it was clear that the men pursuing Gwyn and Iolo had withdrawn.

Glyndyfrdwy

Lord Owain called for a stretcher for the wounded Gwyn and told his men to collect the bodies of the men Gwyn had fought to see if he could get any information from them, but they were both dead.

Lord Owain turned to Iolo and beckoned for him to follow him into the manor. Iolo followed his master into the hall. A servant was sent for food and drink and Iolo was bade to sit beside the fire although he was still soaked from his dunking in the moat. He stood in front of the fire and it soon had his clothes steaming.

Iolo opened his shirt and took out a sealed letter and handed it to Lord Owain, who looked at the seal and then broke it and unfolded the parchment. He read the Latin script and sighed. He crossed to his table where other documents lay strewn and pulled another document out from a pile of papers and held it up.

Iolo could see the document had the king's seal on it.

"It's a summons from the king commanding me to join him in his campaign against the Scots. One of de Grey's men delivered it this morning. I should have received it over a week ago, but now there is not a chance of me getting to the rendezvous on time with all my men and equipment. It's just another of Lord de Grey's stratagems to blacken my name with the king."

"I'm sorry, my lord, I got delayed getting here and I wouldn't be here at all if it hadn't been for Gwyn."

"I take it he's the man who covered your back coming across the field and the moat." Lord Owain paused as Iolo nodded his agreement. "You're a week late. So, tell me, what happened?"

Iolo recounted what had happened to Caradoc and his journey home after the raid into Shropshire. He related the tale of his journey after leaving Ednyfed's farm in the Severn Valley and of the ambush on the way into Bala. He showed Lord Owain the gold he had found in his ambusher's pouch.

Iolo described the ambush and said, "If Gwyn hadn't arrived, I'd be dead. He's been a good friend and travelling companion. I am sorry he got wounded but I had to get the message through to you."

"So de Grey achieved his objective by a message delayed," said the lord, staring wearily into the fire. Iolo watched him. He was deep in thought, and looked as if the world rested upon his shoulders. He was being taken down a road he did not want to go. de Grey had outmanoeuvred him this time and he was not going to let that happen again.

"What do we do now, my lord?" asked Iolo.

"We wait to see the king's response to my letter explaining why I was not at the rendezvous. If he blames de Grey then we join him. However, if he doesn't accept my excuses then we'll have to think of something else." Lord Owain seemed resigned to waiting to hear the king's verdict which he was sure would go against him. de Grey had been working to discredit him for a long time and it looked as if this time he had succeeded.

There was a knock at the door and a man entered. He looked like an exact replica of his older brother. "We've cleared the forest and they have gone. We found the body of an archer with an arrow in his chest. He was carrying this." He held up a hunting horn.

"This was no random attack, it was planned. We found tracks of where the archer was hiding. He's been waiting for at least a week," said Tudor, Owain's younger brother.

"Have you searched him to see if he's working for de Grey?"

"He had these in his pouch, if that's what you mean." Tudor opened his hand to reveal several golden florins, the same as the ones Iolo had just shown Lord Owain.

"I don't think there can be any doubt where they came from. Can you get John Puleston and the Hanmers and send a messenger to the dean of St Asaph that I would like to see him as soon as possible."

Lord Owain turned back to the fire and Tudor left the hall.

Gwyn woke with a pain in his side. He was lying in a bed and his ribs felt as though they had been smashed in by a poleaxe. He lay still, taking in the room with its tapestries of hunting scenes. He wiggled his toes and felt his ribs with his hands. He had been bandaged and his clothes removed. It was then he remembered the flight across the mountains and the charge through the woods to the manor house of the Welsh lord, Iolo's princeling.

His left side hurt from where the horseman's blade had cut him so he rolled onto his right and tried to slide off the bed. He slithered onto his knees and used his hands to get to his feet, supporting some of his weight on his hands. Pain seared through him but he persevered and got to the wall where he leaned for support until the pain partially subsided. He felt light-headed and was in no fit state to travel but he needed to make his way back to the Severn Valley where his reward awaited. Rory would have to pay well for the information he now had.

Gwyn looked round the room and saw that his weapons and clothes were neatly piled neatly on a chest near the window. He started to walk to them but the pain came back, driving him to his knees. So he crawled over to where his belongings were piled. He checked his pouch and his belt and everything was there. He grasped his poniard, drawing it from its scabbard. Gwyn sat with his back to the chest, his legs straight out in front of him. *How am I going to get home?* he mused, reviewing his situation.

The door burst open and a large woman appeared, followed by Iolo. "What do you think you're doing? Are you trying to kill yourself?" she demanded as she lifted him back onto the bed.

"I was just trying to get my things," he said weakly as he tried to rise. "I have to get back home. I am expected back by the end of the month."

"You'll stay in bed until you're told otherwise," snapped the woman. "You tell him," she snapped at Iolo, who had followed her into the room.

"You'd better do as she says or we'll both be in even more trouble," said Iolo as he sat in a chair by the bed. "You need to rest and recover. Lord Owain's surgeon sewed you back together but the sword cut is quite deep and if you don't stay put you'll probably break the stitches and bleed to death. You lost a lot of blood and the prince wants to talk to you. So just lie back and enjoy his lordship's hospitality, I don't expect it will last very long."

"What do you mean the prince? Is Henry of Monmouth here?" gasped Gwyn as he winced in pain.

"No, Lord Owain has declared himself Prince of Wales. The message I was carrying was from John Trefor, the Bishop of St Asaph. It was to warn Lord Owain about how Lord de Grey has been working on the king to declare Lord Owain a traitor. He's been very devious and now the king has issued a summons to arms to Lord Owain but Lord de Grey didn't deliver it, so Lord Owain has been declared a traitor. So Owain's decided with the support of the Hanmers to take Wales back from the English by force."

Gwyn lay back, not quite able to take in what Iolo had told him. It was now even more imperative that he got home because Wales was now at war.

The End

Author's note

I have tried to keep the story in historical context with what was happening at the time in Wales. All errors are mine and mine alone.

The message Iolo carried from John Trefor, Bishop of St Asaph – a warning that the summons had been issued to Owain Glyn Dwr, Lord of Glyndyfrdwy, to join King Henry IV on his campaign to Scotland – is my invention.

The actual summons was sent to Owain Glyn Dwr via Lord Reginald de Grey of Ruthin, who saw that he could take advantage and discredit Owain in the eyes of the king by delaying the delivery of the king's summons.

When Lord de Grey finally delivered the summons Owain Glyn Dwr, an esquire of the Earl of Arundel, did not have time to muster his men and join the king at the meeting place for the army. Owain sent messages to the king complaining about the short notice that he had been given and that it was impossible for him to meet the king's summons.

Lord de Grey told the king that Owain had held the king's summons *in contempt*, and this resulted in the king condemning Owain as a traitor, which led to the Welsh rebellion in September 1400. The Welsh actually caused Henry IV far more trouble than the Scots did for the rest of his reign.

John Trefor, the Bishop of St Asaph, spoke on Owain's behalf in parliament but to no avail and Lord de Grey annexed some of

Owain's lands. Henry IV, the King, had held lands in Brecon but did not understand the Welsh and therefore allowed his marcher lords free reign to deal with the Welsh, which was a big mistake. However, it did give the king's son, the future Henry V, the chance to learn how to be a general. This training was put to good use in his campaigns in northern France when he came to the English throne.

When Henry V came to the throne he sent the earl of Arundel to hand out pardons to all the Welsh bowmen who had fought for Owain Glyn Dwr so that he could recruit them for his campaigns in France.

Henry V had also learned his warfare against the Welsh and this gave him a respect for the men from the principality who managed to hold the English at bay for years and beat them in the two pitched battles between the Welsh and English armies. These battles of Hyddgen and Pilleth are rarely mentioned in English history.

Lord de Grey lost his money when he had to pay a ransom after being captured by Owain Glyn Dwr and he eventually sold his Ruthin estate to Henry Tudor.

Acknowledgements

I would like to thank various people for their help in writing this novel.

First is Mindy Gibbins-Klein who persuaded me that it was worth publishing it, as it was originally written solely for my amusement.

Charlie Wilson for her editing and getting my prose into a fit sate to be read.

David Pugh, for his encouragement and advice. See you in the Wagon for a pint.

Mary, my sister, for her constant belief in me.

Sebastian and Owain, for their constant disbelief.

And last but not least Mandy, my wife, who thinks my writing is a complete waste of time.

Characters

Caradoc | A Welsh traveller returning from Oxford
Ednyfed | Caradoc's father
Mags | Ednyfed's wife
Owain | Caradoc's younger brother

Huw | Ednyfed's brother, Caradoc's uncle
Iolo | Man in Ednyfed's raiding party
Gwillym | Man in Ednyfed's raiding party
Rhodri | Man in Ednyfed's raiding party
Dafydd | Man in Ednyfed's raiding party

Lord Rhys ap Hywel | Welsh lord based in Montgomeryshire
Ieuan | Sergeant in the service of Lord Rhys

Tegwyn	Welsh knight in the service of Lord Rhys
Rory	Rhys's man-at-arms and spy
Gwyn Mochyn	A thief and spy in the employ of Lord Rhys
Ifor ap Goronwy	Bowyer and fletcher from Newtown
Edwin the smith	Blacksmith and armourer
Lord Reginald de Grey	A marcher lord
Gaspard	Sergeant in Lord de Grey's service
Jorge	Sergeant in Lord de Grey's service
Eric	A Saxon who takes over as a Sergeant in Lord de Grey's service
David and Rhys	Welsh speakers in Lord de Grey's service
Owain ap Gruffydd Fychan	Owain Glyn Dwr, Lord of Glyndyfrdwy
Squire to the earl of Arundel	
Tudor ap Gruffydd Fychan	Brother of Owain Glyn Dwr
Bowmen in Lord de Grey's Service	
William	An older archer
Jared	Archer

Earl of Arundel	
Thomas Arundel	Bishop of Canterbury
Chancellor of the Exchequer	
Glyn	Tavern landlord in Clun
Hari	Landlord of The Checkers inn in Newtown
Huw	Landlord of The Red Lion in Dinas Mawddwy
Rhodri	Landlord of the inn in Bala
Eleri	Barmaid at the inn in Bala
Madoc Mawr	Horse trader in Dinas Mawddwy
Eirian	Madoc's brother
Sir Edmund Mortimer	Uncle of the earl of March
Edmund Mortimer	Earl of March, held as a hostage by Henry IV
Will	Farmer on land belonging to the Mortimers
Kate	Will's wife
Robert	Guard at Ludlow Castle

Medieval glossary

Ballinger   English sailing barge, usually with from forty to fifty oars, shallow-draughted and clinker built

Barbican   Fortified gatehouse with tower above or flanked by towers

Bassinet   Conical helmet with hounskul pointed visor

Bastille   Wooden tower on wheels for assault, used in siege warfare

Bastion   Round or polygon tower projecting from the walls

Bombard   Heavy cannon used in siege warfare, firing gun-stones or metal cannon balls of up to a thousand pounds

Bowyer   Bow maker

Brigantine   Defensive jacket of metal plates on cloth

Brimstone   Sulphur

Calthrop	Small metal ball with four angled projecting spikes placed on the battlefield to maim horses
Chevauchee	Military raid through enemy held territory, for the purpose of causing terror and gaining plunder, not much different to the raids of the Vikings. It was a strategy to provoke the enemy into battle or at least weaken his resources and powers of resistance if no battle were offered.
Carrack	Large square rigged sailing vessel of Genoese origin, clinker built
Champion	Officer charged with defending his lord's cause in trial by battle
Cog	Main type of square rigged sailing vessel in use in north European waters, clinker built
Crown	French gold coin weighing 3.99 gm (weights fluctuated) worth twenty and a half sols
Crenel	The space between merlons (see below) on a battlemented wall, also known as an embrasure
Culverin	Light cannon firing lead and bronze bullets, mounted on a portable rest and the ancestor to the hand gun and the harquebus
Cutana	The sword 'curtana' was the pointless sword of mercy (as opposed to the pointed sword of justice) borne before the English king at his coronation
Destrier	Warhorse
Donjon	Keep of a castle

Falchion	Form of heavy straight-bladed sword with a single cutting edge. The blade broadening rather than narrowing towards the tip.
Fascines	A **fascine** is a rough bundle of brushwood used for strengthening an earthen structure, or making a path across uneven or wet terrain. Such bundles were used in military defences for revetting (shoring up) trenches or ramparts, especially around artillery batteries, or filling in ditches. Military fascine bridges were used as early as Roman times.
Fletcher	Arrow maker
Haro	Cry to a lord for rescue
Havoc	The word announcing permission for the troops to plunder
Jack	Defensive leather coat, either of several layers or quilted, often reinforced with metal studs or plates
Jupon	Short leather jacket worn over chain mail
Keep	The strongest single element of a castle, capable of independent defence, generally a tower of wood or stone
Kledyv	An ancient Welsh short sword about two feet in length
Mangonel	Siege engine firing stone shot

March	Borderland – a 'marcher lord' was a lord of a frontier territory, as in Wales where he had considerable independence
Maul	Or mallet – a hammer type weapon, with a heavy leaden head on a five-foot wooden shaft
Merlon	Solid upright part of a battlemented parapet offering shelter to a soldier on the wall walk
Mine	Tunnel dug under foundations of a wall or tower
Misercorde	Mercy dagger, so called from being used to despatch enemy wounded
Morning star	Form of mace, consisting of a spiked ball attached by chain to a short metal shaft
Noble	Principal gold coin of English currency, worth 6s 8d (£0.33)
Patis	Protection money levied by troops on the local population
Pavise	Large free-standing shield on a hinged support used by archers and crossbowmen as protection when shooting
Poleaxe	Combined axe and half pike, with the axe blade balanced by a hammer head on a five-foot wood or metal shaft
Poundage	Customs duty on all imports and exports except bullion
Pourpoint	Quilted doublet

Provost	Royal officer responsible for overseeing the administration of justice
Ribeaudequin	Cart mounting several small culverins discharged together
Sullet	Type of helmet, unattached to neck armour and without a visor
Saltpetre	Potassium nitrate, component of gunpowder
Salut	Lancastrian French equivalent of a gold crown
Sol	Silver or base metal coin (later known as a sou) subdivided into twelve deniers
Sollerets	Articulated armour for feet
Sow	Mobile shelter used in siege warfare, with a strong timber roof and covered in damp hides to make it fireproof
Trebuchet	Siege engine or catapult for hurling rocks or barrels of flaming tow, the principal form of heavy artillery before the bombard and afterward used as supplementary cannon
Tunnage	Customs duty on wine imported in casks, levied at so much per ton

Places and castles

Bala Lake
Clun Castle
Dolforwyn Castle

Glyndyfrdwy   Moated manor house of Owain Glyn Dwr
Ludlow Castle
Montgomery Castle

Newtown was originally the hamlet of Llanfair yng Nghedewain or the church of St Mary in Cedewain. However it is now been translated into Drenewydd

Shrewsbury Castle
Shrewsbury Abbey

Vale of Ceri

Bibliography

Dolforwyn Castle, Montgomery Castle
    CADW

Glyn Dwr's War
    GJ Brough

Owain Glyn Dwr and the War of Independence in the Welsh Borders
    Geoffrey Hodges, Penguin, 1988

Long Bow
    Robert Hardy

The Medieval Archer
    Bradbury

Ludlow Castle – Its History and Buildings
    Shoesmith and Johnson

Printed in the United Kingdom
by Lightning Source UK Ltd.
132035UK00002B/1-66/P